Trent Mullins holds the bottle of pills that .... climb out of the black hole that nearly killed him. Tossing the bottle over the Wrightsville Beach Drawbridge, he feels the first sliver of light in months.

He leaves family, friends, and the area that had served as his home for his entire life. With the help of his best friend, Jackson, he lands in the coastal area of Georgia. A new job, unlikely landlords, and the peaceful marshlands that serve as his front yard slowly bring a measure of stillness to his troubled mind.

But then an unwelcome phone call mandates his return home to bury the father he never knew and to face the son he left behind.

Praise for Home, Billy Beasley's Latest Work

"Navigating the gamut of human relationships is never easy, particularly in the South, where the undercurrent of racism simmers below the surface, but Billy Beasley has written a suspenseful story that keeps you enthralled and doesn't let go until the very last page."—**Kathryn Gauci, USA Today bestselling author**

"If the first chapter doesn't give you a lot to think about then you weren't paying attention! It sets the stage for a homecoming that will surely be eventful. If the rest of the book is anything like the first chapter I won't get any sleep until I finish it."—**Herman Dickens, Avid Reader**

"Beasley's characters are as natural, intriguing, and as full of life as the Carolina coast they call home. Their conflicts play out in a low country Eden that is as stirring and primal as the passions of its people."—*Joseph McSpadden, Host of the Village Night Owl Podcast and Contributing Editor, Okra Magazine*

"Billy does a brilliant job making his characters come to life. He is not afraid to tackle racial injustices, political corruption, while incorporating his faith. His writing style is reminiscent of my favorite southern author, Pat Conroy. Billy's stories are gripping, raw and oh so believable."—*Helen Johnson Brumbaugh, Retired Interior Designer*

"Billy Beasley has become my favorite author. His first novel, *The River Hideaway,* should be made into a movie. I read the opening chapter of *Home* and cried tears of joy with the characters I was introduced to. This southern author pulls his readers hearts and souls into his characters and the inviting marshlands he portrays so vividly that I felt I could see, smell, almost touch it."—*Wylene Booth McDonald, Retired Merck & Company*

"Billy Beasley has done it once again! With his latest work 'Home,' Beasley has created characters that resonate within the soul and are relatable, despite their flaws. Once you pick up this book you will not want to put it down until you have finished it. I highly recommend *Home*"—*Todd Osborne, Avid Reader*

Billy Beasley's heartwarming novels are

are starting to draw National Attention.

"*The Girl In The River* allowed me to visit a place I love, that made me who I am, every time I opened its pages. The story is a testament to the human spirit and the true nature of the people of my home state. As Josie shows, there is no more loyal love than that from a dog."

LARA TRUMP
FOX NEWS CONTRIBUTOR

More Praise for *The Girl in the River*

"Billy Beasley has done it again...I started this book and couldn't put it down until the story was completed. Billy Beasley's stories are soul searching and keep us evaluating our contributions to life. An awesome storyteller. I patiently await his next book, *Home.*"—*Mary Poole, Avid Reader*

"I loved "The Girl In The River" so, so much. I so enjoy how the author lays the story out in the first part to the book to prepare the reader for quite an intriguing second half, filled with a roller coaster of emotions. I cried so hard as I read the last part of the book....tears of joy and tears of sadness. Brilliant, Billy Beasley!!"—*Dr. Johnnie Sexton*

Acknowledgments

Jack Humphrey, for the book cover shot and your constant encouragement and for always being there. Thanks for playing the main character's best friend in *Home.*

For those of you who buy multiple copies, write reviews, tell your friends, and always believe in my ability to spin a story. Thank you from the bottom of my heart.

Julie and Teke.

Don & Jan Morgan, who not only gave their blessing to my marrying their daughter. They took Micah and I into their family and have loved us as their own.

Gene, and the staff at Moonshine Cove Publishing. You make me a better writer.

For Micah Brooks Beasley, the main character in this story often feels unworthy of his wonderful son. I know just how he feels.

Kim,
Great book club.
Psalm 40:2
Billy Beasley

HOME

Billy Beasley

Moonshine Cove Publishing, LLC

Abbeville, South Carolina U.S.A.

First Moonshine Cove Edition April 2022

ISBN: 9781952439292

Library of Congress LCCN: 2022904428

© Copyright 2022 by Billy Beasley

About the Author

Billy's first novel, *The River Hideaway,* was published in April, 2014.

Billy was determined to be published and weathered many  rejections along the way. It was in 2013, when his new wife, Julie, asked when was the last time he had tried to get published. It had been a few years. He randomly selected one publisher and sent the story out to appease her. Later that year, he was offered a contract for *The River Hideaway,* a story he began in 1998. *The Preacher's Letter,* his second published novel, was released in January of 2018. *The Girl in the River* was published in July of 2020.

Billy is always more engaged to write stories than to tackle the arduous task of finding a publisher who would say yes. He has completed manuscripts resting in his computer that he hopes to see in print one day.

Billy resides in Carolina Beach, North Carolina, with his beautiful wife and biggest supporter, Julie and their Australian Cattle Dog, Teke, who graciously agreed to play the role of Josie in *The Girl in the River.*

https://www.billybeasley.com

Author's Note

Dylan Town is a fictional community and comprised of people who only exist in the writer's imagination.

HOME

1

The initial morning rays of the sun flickered inside my bedroom, stirring me gently awake. Hesitantly, I reached across the bed, finding the presence of no one. She had departed, and for that, I was more than grateful.

I stretched my long body across the entire bed, enjoying the freedom, if not the surplus of perfume left behind on the linens. I glanced at my watch. It was a few minutes past seven. Work began at ten. I smiled lazily and returned quickly to a deep slumber.

Within minutes I was dreaming. It was one of those dreams that failed to make sense. There was a constant revolving of characters. I recognized some people, while others, I was confident that I had never laid eyes upon. That proved a mystery to me. How could strangers visit your dreams?

Elton John sang, "Don't Let the Sun Go Down on Me," joining my dream. It took several moments to realize that it was, in actuality, the ring tone on my cell phone. Lazily, I searched for my phone, recognizing that this was real life. Whatever the hell constituted that these days.

The owner of the marina, Howard, my employer, was vacationing in Greece. That ruled him out. He was having too much fun with his tall, thin, blonde, air-headed mistress, who was probably half his age. That left only two other people with access to my phone number, and one of them just departed.

I reached for the backpack on the floor. I pulled the phone out and punched the button and feigned anger. "Jackson, it's a little early."

There was a long pause before I heard a voice. "Trent, it's Linda."

Linda was the youngest of my four older sisters.

"Daddy is dying."

My first thought was to offer something humorous like, "You have pronounced him dead for years," which she had, but I refrained. There was something in her tone that tells me that this might not be the best time for my particular brand of wit, which my family never quite fully appreciated. They failed to understand me on any matters. It proved easier, I suspect in most families, to place inaccurate labels on the members in our family and never remove them. To eradicate those labels would be to admit being wrong, and beginning at the top with my father, that was not a characteristic that ran rampant through the Mullins family. I did not catch that trait from my father as I have spent most of my life trying to be anything but like him. I did well in my endeavor with the exception of inheriting a large dosage of his legendary impatience.

Don't misunderstand. I valued my father's influence greatly. I learned much from him in reverse. I saw how he behaved. How he craved being the center of attention. How he never really listened to anyone. He had two things on his mind. What he was saying and what he planned to say next. He could never acknowledge any of his failings. I never heard the man offer a single apology to any of his children. And believe me, he had much to express regret for.

"How long does he have?"

"It's hard to tell."

"What does the doctor say?"

"Not a damn thing." There was anger and sadness in her voice. I heard sniffling, and I know that she was crying through her indignation.

My father had endured two open-heart surgeries and lived in a constant state of congestive heart failure. Several times he was rushed to the emergency room, seemingly always in the dead of night. Each time, he survived, much to the astonishment of the family.

Linda composed herself. "They just released him from the hospital after he stayed for a week. The doctors told us the first day he had pneumonia, and today they discharged him and said basically nothing. If they sent him home to die, they could have at least told us."

"Maybe it's not that bad."

There was silence, and I knew that my response was not the correct one. That was to be expected. I am the baby brother of four much older sisters and the only son of an overbearing father.

"Well then, why don't you remain in whatever hole you ran away to, you miserable bastard." She ended the call abruptly.

"That went well," I declared, tossing my phone on the bed.

Linda could go weeks without cursing, but when irritated, she spewed obscenity as gracefully as an inmate on a chain gang. She had just been adequately provoked.

I contemplated my next move. I retrieved my phone and walked outside onto the deck. It was low tide, and there was marsh grass, mud, and several pockets of water that have formed a rock's throw in front of me. Beyond the initial marsh grass, there was a narrow creek that eventually made its way to and from the East River.

I breathed in the pungent odors of the land in front of me. The wind gently swayed the plentiful grasses of the marsh. Directly in front of me, there were three great blue herons, to my left, several snowy egrets. They were busy foraging the marsh. A Ring-billed gull rested on an old round piling, which held a sign so rusted, with letters so faded, that I had never been able to ascertain what was written on it. Behind me, there was a patch of woods. The trees were mostly oak, and they are kept in check with salt spray. Most had crooked trunks and gnarled limbs. The underbrush was thick, and only a fool would try to navigate through it. A lone dirt road, maybe three football fields long led to this place where I have resided for nearly two years. It was a small two-bedroom, one-bath house-constructed over one hundred years ago. It was obviously built well to have stood the test of the many storms that have battered the east coast.

It was quiet and peaceful, and it helped calm the demons that so viciously ravaged my mind not so long ago.

I called my best friend, Jackson Humphrey.

"Good morning, sunshine," he answered. "Coming home?"

"See you this afternoon."

"Your room will be ready," he said.

We ended the call without saying goodbye.

I heard the rhythmic tapping that occurred each morning of late. There was a decaying pine tree with little bark remaining to my left. A beautiful red-headed woodpecker pecked away for breakfast.

"Good morning, Marty." He continued tapping without acknowledging that I had spoken. I moved my eyes away from him and gazed at the scenery around me. My thoughts drifted to the period that ultimately led me to this hole, as my sister had so aptly depicted it.

***

I was kayaking soon after moving to the area. I got caught in an unexpected thunderstorm. The thunder was rolling and it kept building to a deafening boom. Lightning flashed all around me. The heavens opened all at once, and the rain descended so hard that my vision was limited to a few feet. There seemed to be no safe haven to ride out the storm, and I was not a fan of staying in the water with the electric charges of the lightning so fierce that the hairs on my arms stood straight up. I caught a glimpse of light, and I paddled toward it. My kayak found purchase on a small expanse of sandy shoreline. I ran to the little house and knocked on the door. No one answered. I gazed into a small window and saw no one. I went back to the door and turned the old black metal doorknob, and to my surprise, it opened. I cautiously stepped inside and called out, "Hello. Is anyone home?" I heard nothing. I saw the electric candle in another window that had led me out of the storm. Guardedly, I walked through the house. I was relieved to find no one. It contained sparse furniture, and the kitchen had a few cooking items and some canned goods. It did not appear to be lived in.

The storm moved past quickly, and the sky was without clouds in a few minutes. I pulled my kayak back into the water and continued my journey.

During that time, I was temporarily staying in a condo that Howard and his wife, Brenda, owned. It was proving claustrophobic. I asked Howard about the shack that I discovered in the storm, and he bellowed with laughter. "Son, you don't want to live there. That shack is owned by a black couple that runs a store in the community. There are no white people living in that area. Bad idea."

I persisted and he gave me directions to the store. It was the following day when the paved road I drove upon turned to gravel. A weathered wooden sign read, Dylan Town, "Population, It Varies." Behind the sign was a gigantic live oak that appeared to be sixty feet high, with a spread of over one hundred feet. Spanish moss clung to the branches on the north side.

The first building was an old white clapboard church, set back in the distance. The grounds were well kept, and the church appeared as if it had just been painted. There was a steeple, with a large bronze church bell residing below it.

I drove through the community that contained modest homes that, for the most part, were kept very neat. It was afternoon as I approached the store. The first part of the building was a screened-in area. I opened the weathered screen door and walked in. One side had a sign that read produce-the other, seafood. Both were empty. There was a sign to my right that read. If you didn't catch it or grow it here. We don't want it.

There was a wooden sign above the next door, which was also wooden and painted a dark gray. The words Dylan's Grille was routed and burned into the sign. I took a deep breath and entered. Three older black gentlemen were sitting in brown, worn wood rockers in the corner, gathered around a large wooden spool that was the color of an old barn. Two of the men studied the chessboard that rested between them. The other man smoked a pipe and occasionally peered intently at the board and shook his head as if he was privy to information the players were not. They all seemed to notice me simultaneously, and in unison, they cocked their head to the left and constricted their faces in either amusement or astonishment. I couldn't speak as to which.

There were two long sections of shelving that contained canned goods, snacks, a few basic over the counter medications, and some fishing supplies. An old soft drink container-the type that you pushed the glass back and reached down to select the soft drink of your choice.

To my right, a more modern cooler stood against the wall that contained eight different types of beer and three kinds of wine. An old Falstaff sign hung crookedly above the cooler.

There were six square wooden tables toward the back of the store. The napkin holder and condiments all spaced precisely the same on each table. Four chairs tucked neatly under the tables.

I heard soft conversation and moved toward its source. I walked to the counter, where a black man of impressive size was cleaning the grill. He wore denim overalls with a short sleeve white tee shirt underneath that fought to contain his massive arms. Beside him, a lady wiped down the counter. She wore a red checkered dress. A white apron was tied around the back of her neck and waist. They talked softly with each other. I cleared my throat and said, "Excuse me."

They both turned around. He tightened his eyes. "Whatever it is, we are not buying," he declared firmly in a gravelly voice, before dismissing me as he turned back to the task at hand.

A smart man would have just walked away, but no one had ever accused me of being overly intelligent. I am a shade over six feet tall and I weigh two-hundred-twenty pounds. I lift weights and run several times weekly, but this man appeared as if he could pick me up and throw me the length of the store. Still, I had come a long way. "I am not selling anything."

He started to speak, and I observed the lady still him with a slight grip of her hand on top of his forearm. "What is it you want, honey?"

She was an attractive lady, medium height, and full-figured. Her eyes were wide and expressive, and she reminded me of the actor, Alfre Woodard.

"The place you have through the woods. Do you rent it?"

He looked agitated, and he was about to speak, but she had not yet released his forearm.

"I'm sorry, ma'am. I forgot my manners. My name is Trent. Trent Mullins."

She let go of his arm and extended her hand. "I am Maybelle Dylan. That is Maybelle and not Mabel," she stated very business-like with additional emphasis on the last syllable, and this is my husband, Moses." When Moses did not move swiftly enough to greet me, she stated steadfastly without room for debate. "Shake his hand, Moses."

His hand engulfed mine with power. He held it a little longer than necessary. As he released my hand, she looked perplexed as she asked, "Why would you want to live out there all isolated?"

"It's a long story, ma'am."

She waited, but I was not offering my narrative to anyone.

"Probably running from the law," Moses said under his breath as he turned back to the grill.

She smacked him with her cleaning towel. Not hard, but firm enough that I heard a little snap.

He turned back around and narrowed his face. She placed her hands on her hips and arched her eyebrows as if he were a small child that needed reprimanding.

"We are trying to finish up here and get out of this store. We close at two sharp every day, and if you will notice, it is five minutes to two," he said, as he pointed to an old round clock that had Frostie Root Beer written in cursive across the middle of it.

I followed his hand and smiled faintly as I admired the weathered clock. When I turned back to face him, he was studying me.

I shrugged my shoulders. "When I was a kid, I loved root beer, and that one was my favorite." I paused before continuing. "I was kayaking one day when I saw the place. I stopped and looked around. I could tell no one was living there. I asked my boss about it, and he told me that you were the owners." I omitted the part where I ventured inside without permission.

"Who is your boss?"

"Howard Beck. He owns the boatyard in Brunswick that I manage for him."

"And what did he say when you asked him about living in that old shack?"

"He laughed."

He studied me for a moment. I think he expected me to sugarcoat things, and he was not sure what to make of me right now. That's okay. I felt the same way each morning I looked in the mirror.

He glared at me intently, and then he began counting things off on his long thick fingers. "No central heating and air. No air condition period. No cable. No phone. No WIFI. Power is about all you have, and that is limited. You can't drink the water, and you can barely stand to shower in it." He turned to Maybelle. "Did I leave anything out? Oh," he said, answering his own question as he snapped his fingers loudly. "No white people."

I studied him for a few moments. I felt a slight smile escaping, even as I fought to suppress it.

"Something funny?" he inquired, not sharing in my amusement.

"Obviously, you sell things for a living, and it appears to me that you might just be going about it the wrong way."

His eyes widened, and he was about to respond, but her hand was back on his arm, and then she laughed heartily. "Man got a point, Moses. Man, surely got a point indeed."

"When would you want to move in?" she asked.

"Yesterday," I replied wearily.

"Where are you living now, and how long have you been working for Mr. Beck?"

"I just started working for him recently, and he is letting me live in one of his rental condos. I can't stand it. I feel like I can't breathe." I sighed deeply. "It is indeed a long story of how I landed here. I moved from Wilmington. I just needed something that wasn't familiar. I won't cause you any trouble. I will pay the rent ahead of time and in cash. Oh, and I'm not running from the law," I added as I shifted my eyes to Moses.

"Five hundred a month," she said. "That's for everything. The stove and hot water heater run on gas. Try to keep the bill down."

I nodded as I pulled the stone-colored slim wallet from the front pocket of my tan cargo shorts. I counted off five one-hundred-dollar bills from the money clip inside the wallet.

"May I move in tomorrow?"

She nodded.

"Do I need to sign a lease?"

"Is your word good?"

"Yes, ma'am. It's about all I have left that is."

"Mine is as well," she said, extending her hand. I grasped it and said, "Thank you, ma'am."

"Maybelle," she said.

"Maybelle," I repeated.

As I walked away, I overheard Moses remark to his wife. "I got a bad feeling about this."

2

I placed my coffee mug in the sink. Next, I called Howard's wife, Brenda, and informed her that I had a family emergency back home, and that I would be departing immediately. She was not pleased, and I don't care. I offered no additional information about what occurrence necessitated my need to leave town. She could agonize about running the marina. It can't be that hard. I manage to do it.

I packed a few clothes into a large duffel bag. There were only casual clothes to pack because that was all that I possessed here in the hole that I ran away to as my sister so succinctly stated. If there was a funeral to attend my lone suit hung in the closet of my old bedroom in the simple brick ranch that I grew up in. I grabbed the book that rested on the nightstand. *The Death of Santini,* by Pat Conroy, and added it to the bag.

I drove through the woods until the scenery opened. I navigated the wooden bridge with a small creek running underneath. Essentially, I lived on a small island. But it was not the type of luxury one might equate with island living. The house was built before building codes existed in the area. It was not insured, and I suspected that there would be no rebuilding if it was ever marred severely.

The power came from Dylan's Grille. I lived in one of the few residences in the United States that lacked air conditioning, a television, or a computer.

During the sweltering nights of summer, I relied on fans and prayed for coastal winds to blow through the windows. The winters were mild, and the temperatures rarely dipped below thirty degrees. There was an efficient wood stove in the living room and kitchen area that easily heated the entire house when necessary.

I stopped at the first building. There was a rusted Esso Gas sign by two pumps that are the color of faded brick and rust. The pumps had not worked in years.

I liked the store even if Moses was not fond of his only Caucasian customer, as he often stated, but I had hope. I told Maybelle once that I was growing on him. He overheard and said, "Yeah, like a bad fungus."

Regardless of how he felt about me, I couldn't help but admire two people who worked so hard to earn a living. Moses, one day, while in the midst of talking up a blue streak for the likes of him, said, "I do this because my father did it, and his father before him, and his father before that."

They woke early six days a week to begin their day, and the door closed at two each afternoon. Sundays are a reminder of what the South once was. The store was closed, and as Maybelle liked to say, "That is churching day."

There was an old faded Pepsi sign on the wall. Maybelle once shared that Moses discovered that Pepsi's distributor had been charging him more than the white store owners in town. He told him to take his merchandise and leave. The unwise man offered some callus remarks as he packed up. Maybelle was narrowly able to coax her husband to refrain from breaking the bigoted man in half.

I continued walking to the back of the store. They served sausage and bacon biscuits for breakfast, which were so good they made you want to slap your mama. That was what Moses once told me. They were delicious, but I never desired to slap my mama. It was yet another one of those southern sayings that confused the northerners that kept moving to the south in droves, and to be frank, as southern as I am, there were still sayings I can't comprehend. For lunch, the choices were cheeseburgers, chicken, ham sandwiches and french fries. Each Saturday, they offered pulled pork sandwiches, topped in Maybelle's slaw. They were the best barbeque sandwiches that I had ever tasted.

Each Saturday, Moses smoked a pig while the rest of us slept. It was worth the effort from my perspective, and though I worked most Saturdays, especially during the warmer months, Maybelle had been known to hold back a couple of sandwiches for their sole white patron.

There was a couple that appeared to be in their early thirties, eating breakfast at one of the tables. She wore a red University of Georgia football tee shirt. The man had a similar shirt but in black. They looked at me with a peculiar expression, but the woman gave me a slightly curious but somewhat flirtatious look. I moved my eyes quickly away from her and in the direction of Moses.

He was a versatile man in his many talents. When the season was right for it, he would take his small green johnboat out and harvest oysters or clams, which he sold to his customers. He professed that he did not care for the taste of oysters, but when he had a good day digging for clams, clam fritters went on the lunch menu, and I had witnessed him eating a plate so full of them that it looked like you would need a metal tray just to bear the weight.

He worked cleaning the grill as I approached. His shaved head glistened with perspiration. Moses turned sixty earlier this year. Maybelle was fifty-five. They had been married since she was seventeen.

I lifted weights most of my adult life and ate reasonably healthy. On the other hand, Moses, fueled by pork, beef, chicken and fried seafood, had twenty-inch plus arms. He was right at six feet tall, and probably weighed two-fifty, and nearly all of that muscle.

He liked to say he was big from hard work, and that was partially true. But one day, I noticed an old metal shed adjacent to the store with an opening where a garage size door once hung. Inside there was a weight bench and an Olympic barbell that held four big plates. Two hundred and twenty-five pounds. I would discover that was where he began his workout. His warm-up weight exceeded more than most men could even aspire to lift. There were rusted Olympic plates and a few dumbbells scattered about. Maybelle told me the first thing he did after work each Monday and Thursday was to lift weights for an hour. I also witnessed him split a cord of firewood in less than an hour. His routine so fluid and without wasted motion that it reminded me of the water from a small mountain creek flowing around rocks.

He peered up at me and then resumed cleaning the grill. Breakfast was over, and it was transition time to preparing lunch. Maybelle was nowhere to be found. He grunted disgustedly and shook his head.

"Is it too late for me to purchase two sausage biscuits?"

He said nothing as he continued to clean. A minute or more passed as I stood there wondering why he was being less sociable than usual. He turned and walked to the counter that divided us and handed me two sausage and cheese biscuits.

I gave him three dollars, and as he took it, his eyes locked in on mine. "I saw that woman driving that fancy car leaving while it was still dark this morning. You can paint it six ways to Sunday, but you know what you were doing is wrong."

I closed my eyes and nodded my head. He returned to cleaning the grill.

"I'll be gone for a few days."

He failed to respond, and I walked away, knowing I had disappointed yet another person. My list kept growing.

***

"He's gone," Moses said.

Maybelle emerged from the storage room. He shook his head with tiny controlled shakes. "I ought to boot that white boy's ass out of here."

She turned her head to the right, and her face grew stern. "Moses, I won't abide by vulgar talk. And need I remind you that we are all God's children. You need to read 1 Samuel 16:7 again."

"I know. I know. God looks on the heart of a man," he said with a roll of his eyes.

"Maybe it is about time you live it better. And don't you roll those eyes at me, Moses Dylan."

He sighed and shook his head. "That boy's heart is no good."

"That is not for us to judge."

"Why does he come around here anyway? No one around here wants his kind."

She narrowed her eyes. "Why don't you listen to yourself. His kind? Do you remember how you felt when the man from Pepsi was cheating you or all the many times someone disrespected you because of your skin color? Do you think it is okay for you to treat him differently because he's white? You know better, Moses Dylan."

"That is twice you used my last name. No need in getting all riled up."

"You know what you are saying about that boy, who by the way is in his forties, is just plain wrong."

"You should have never allowed him to live here."

"But you don't mind the extra five hundred each month, do you?"

"We got along okay before he came."

"When was the last time anyone wanted to rent that place?"

"I don't know."

"I do. Three years."

Moses resumed cleaning the grill. Several minutes passed before she touched him lightly on the back. He turned to face her. She offered a smile that held a hint of such warmth that it gave his heart pause. "What are your plans when the store closes today?"

"Tide is going to be running. I thought I might see if I can catch us something for dinner."

"Hmm," she offered as she appeared in deep thought.

"Why? What were you thinking?"

"Well, I thought that I would leave work a little early and go home and get myself cleaned up. Maybe stretch out on the bed and wait for someone. But if you would rather fish."

"I can fish another time," he quickly answered.

***

I diverted from making my way to Interstate 95 and drove to a parking lot that bordered the ocean. I parked and walked out onto the beach strand. Soon I would be in another coastal setting. The same Atlantic Ocean but worlds apart for me. I knew at some point that I would have to return. Still, it was one of those journeys in life that I had hoped to somehow conveniently postpone indefinitely.

The sun was bright and interrupted briefly by a few stray fragmented clouds. The surf was chest high, and several surfers were scattered just beyond the break.

I'm not sure what I was supposed to feel about the impending death of my father. He was a good man and a wonderful husband to my mother, but I accepted long ago that we would never share any kind of meaningful relationship. He dictated this path by keeping everyone but my mother at arm's length. It was what he was comfortable with, and it was what felt right for me as well. I have observed so many others chase after a father's approval like it was the winning lottery ticket blowing down the street. I thought about Pat Conroy's book, *The Death of Santini.* His father proved to be a far more abusive parent than my dad, but yet Pat longed for his approval. I could never recall a time when I desired to be close to my father or sought his approval, even as a small child. I tuned him out at a very early age. I have no understanding of what any of this means.

My thoughts drifted to the woman that I once loved without competition. I watched as she cast away our life together to please her father who hated me with unbridled intensity. He was a rich, pompous, arrogant man who spent much of his time projecting and protecting his social image. His positive image excelled only in his eyes. I think everyone else saw him for exactly who he was. Maybe that was his greatest trepidation.

My father desired that I seek his approval and though it was unachievable. I think it offended his pride that this matter held little concern for me. I had watched numerous movies and read many books in which this joyous reconciliation between father and child occurred. I was confident that my father would have none of that, and I was at peace with that. The great divide between us proved comforting to me in some anomalous way. It would seem to be a far greater waste to discover that on his deathbed, he possessed some depth of feeling and chose to ignore it. If this was true, it would mean that he could have spent some of his valuable time caring about what I thought, what I felt, instead of criticizing me for not thinking and viewing life precisely as he did. I don't believe he ever had a poignant moment in which he contemplated life. Maybe it was because his life, for the most part, was exactly the way he desired it. He loved his work as a firefighter, and his other love was my mother. She allowed him the life he desired with minimal interference. It would have been better if that was all that was involved. But through the years, six children were born.

Mom was twenty when she had twin girls. Connie arrived first-followed four minutes and thirty-eight seconds later by Chloe. Two years passed, and then, believe it or not, there was another set of twin girls, Lydia and Linda.

My parents were through having children, or so they thought, but when Mom was thirty-seven, she had twin boys. Roger, named after my dad, died seven days after he was born. I survived despite the many times I wished that it would have been him to live and face this challenging world and not me. I have also often wondered what it might have been like to have a brother.

Four of us have at times expressed in our adult years that we never really felt loved by our father. Only Connie, goes to great lengths to profess his love for her and the family. She neatly absolved him of any wrongdoings. If his memory proved selective, even fabricated, as it habitually was, such as how he took credit for paying or doing things that he never did. It went unchallenged by her. Her rationale was that he would have helped if he could have. The last part was correct, and of that, I had no doubts, but it was not the truth. I tended to see things black and white without varying shades of gray. Maybe if our family had chosen long ago to deal with our unpleasant truths‐ perhaps we might have been the close family that my mom pretended that we were. Possibly, Connie believed that it was the more dignified way to view things as she did. As for me, being dignified was not something that I ever gave a rat's ass about. I refused to grant my father a free pass for the misery he inflicted.

My mother tried in vain to encourage me to see my childhood and our family in the way she would have the world to view it and maybe the way the world perceived us to be. I would not take part in this farce. For my honesty, I was sometimes labeled as angry and perhaps bitter. I found it most amusing that if I would lie and speak of how wonderful my father had been the family would have applauded.

Connie, never once, to my knowledge, challenged our father. For the most part, Linda followed suit, though she would attempt to win Dad over with diplomacy. My other sisters, when properly pushed, would fire back at him with a vengeance. As for me, I would go toe to toe with him like it was Ali-Frazier III.

Little League baseball visited my memories and of how embarrassing he proved to be, hollering at me from the bleachers and trying to entertain those around him with his sad comedic routine.

I chuckled as I recalled a pleasant Little League memory. It was opening day. The game was in extra innings, and our opponent had the bases loaded with two out. The batter hit a sure base hit into center field. To this day, I did not know how I arrived in that spot to make such a catch. Maybe it was one of those times in life when you knew exactly what was happening before it transpired. I don't know how else to explain a small child, playing second base, being well into the outfield to catch a ball that had base hit stamped on it from the moment of contact.

Dad was working, and only Mom was present to witness the catch. I speculated at times whether I would have made that catch if he had been in the stands that night. Maybe I would have been cringing, bracing for him to bellow out unsolicited advice, and not relaxed enough to make the catch of my life. He always proved heavy-handed with the criticism, but there was never any follow through with an offer to assist.

Years later, he shared his version for why a baseball player and a former catcher such as himself never helped me. It was my fault. In his tainted, selective memory, he tried to help, but I was too stubborn to listen. The truth was that he didn't want to be disturbed, and I would have respected that if he would have just been honest. I could count on one hand the times he even played a simple game of catch with me, and he was always waiting for the first opportunity to escape. He once spoke of buying a catcher's mitt to help me with my pitching. But just as the basketball rim that Santa brought one year for Christmas, there was no follow-through. The mitt went unpurchased, and the rim sat in the shed for years. I took it to my friend Rick's house, where we hung it and put it to use. Dad dared to ask why. Gee, I don't know. Perhaps, because it hung in the shed for so long, it showed signs of rust. The foolish kid that I was. I thought when the rim was a present under the tree that it would be up the next week. I asked him to put it up until summer came. He kept saying he would do it during his time off from work, which as a fireman, those days were plentiful.

Someone could tell him this story today, and he would either express no recollection of such an occurrence, or his version would be completely different. One thing for certain, he was not going to be wrong about a basketball rim or any other episode in this life.

As I gazed out at a surfer getting crunched by a wave that he was clearly apprehensive of riding, my mind drifted to the two earliest memories of my youth and then to other defining events in the relationship with my father that proved strained from birth.

There was a harbor on the island of Wrightsville Beach, where large, wooden, commercial fishing boats docked. It was one of my father's hangouts. Sometimes he rode with one of the sea captains on their shorter runs. On this particular day, he took me with him. The only part of the day I recall was what happened when we returned to the docks. He handed me up to another man who was standing on the tattered wood above. During the exchange, he said, "Don't drop him. His mama will kill me if I come home without him."

I could not have been more than five years of age, and why that long-ago memory chose to remain stored in the recesses of my mind, I don't know. Maybe it was because even though each thought of his failed to venture beyond the surface; it indicated what he cared about far more than anything else in this life. My mom.

The other aged recollection was one of being stuck on the porch while my parents argued. "And take this boy with you," Mom said angrily. It was not the words that remained so clearly etched in my mind. It was the agitated look that consumed my father's face. Clearly, he did not want to be bothered with a small boy, but my mother picked few battles with him, and she always emerged the victor when she did. There was a look of resignation, as he took me with him without issuing another word, but he was none too pleased about it, and though I was but a small child, I knew it.

I bore no hardness towards my mom. She was a wonderful woman whose best parenting would be when I was an adult. Maybe, as I would eventually discover it was just a way that I neatly absolved her from any culpability.

My thoughts continued to drift, swirling about like feathers in the wind. I don't recall the circumstances for why, but not long ago, I shared this particular story with Connie and her husband. It was the day my son Brooks' mom and I joined the church my parents attended. At the conclusion of the service, the new members formed a line across the front of the sanctuary, and those who desired to greet them would welcome each new member. There were many hugs offered along the way to the latest additions to the church. My dad had just finished hugging my ex-wife, and before he was in front of me, he said sternly, "Don't hug me, boy."

His fears were unwarranted. I had no intention of embracing him. I knew he was not comfortable hugging any man. Now that I think about it, we never shook hands either. I recalled the horror in Connie's eyes as I shared this story, and though I would never do it, I could tell her a hundred stories far worse than that one.

As the years moved beyond that encounter at church, I reflected mostly with sympathy that a man who desired everyone to think that he was tough was terrified that his son might hug him.

Another story barged into my thoughts. One that had not emerged in decades. My wonderful father did a nice thing back in the summer that I was nine years old. A dog of mixed breed wandered to the fire station where he worked. The dog was male and underweight. They fed it and kept it for a few days, and when it became apparent that no one cared about the dog, my father decided to bring him home as a gift to me.

I was elated. I named him Tony. Three evenings later, I returned home from playing in the neighborhood. I excitedly checked on my new friend. He was gone. I ran into the house and told Linda that Tony was lost and we had to find him. She informed me that dad had visited some friends that day and mentioned the dog. They inquired about Tony and mentioned their last dog had passed away three months prior. Dear old dad drove home and picked Tony up and took him to his friend's house and became their hero by giving them my dog. These people would, without question, be among the many that would paint my father as a wonderful, giving person. I would say that he crushed a little boy's heart, and there was never even a discussion of what became of Tony in the Mullins household. It was just the way things were. The old man decided the course of action with no thought for anyone else, and we were supposed to line up, salute, and say, "Thank you, sir. May I have another portion of the shit you repetitively heap on us?"

My phone vibrated with a spam call. I pressed end and noticed that the screen showed April. It had done so seemingly without my knowledge. There was a time not too distant that the beginning of April would have produced hope and joy. The following month was once my favorite because as I relaxed on the beach, basking in the sunshine, I would comfort myself with the knowledge that there was six good months of beach season ahead. I lived for the summer and loathed the coming of late fall and winter.

I no longer venerated the summer or detested the winter. The seasons have somehow lost their intimacy. One month seemed like any other, be it the sweltering heat of July or the damp, dreary, grayness of January.

I watched one dream after another disperse into oblivion. I cursed my bad luck, my bad choices, and I never could get past thinking that God was up there toying with me.

Maybe I could not think healthy thoughts of God because I could never entirely escape the Southern Baptist Church teachings drilled into me as a young boy. I remembered little if anything from the long-winded instructions. Still, I can't shake the image of this gigantic figure, with a stern look etched on his face, standing in a floorless room in the sky at a blackboard, marking my mistakes down with chalk that never ran out.

Eventually, my mother left the church of her youth to join an Evangelical Presbyterian Church that played lively music and stretched out hands were part of the worship service. It also had members who were not all white. You certainly were not going to find that in the church I grew up in.

As a child, I was taught in church a wonderful song. "Jesus Loves the Little Children". *Yellow, red, or black or white, they are precious in His sight.* Those were great words, but to the church, they were exactly that, just words.

I've strived to find an answer that would explain the life we lead or perhaps that leads us. If something injured me the way the pain numbed me of life when Carmen brutally turned on me to walk the path dictated by her father. I searched for the lesson that would lead me to a better place. It was symbolic of climbing a mountain, struggling to reach the peak where I could finally rest. But there came a time when not only did I fail to near the top, but the starting point seemed to recede farther back. I long ago ceased striving to make sense out of this life.

I had stalled long enough. I walked to my car and began the drive north, leaving Georgia's coast behind.

3

I sat with Mom in a room that once served as a bedroom. It had been many years since children lived in this pale brick home. The room we now occupied served as my father's den. It was his domain, his refuge.

The look in her faded blue eyes reminded me of an early morning July sky. She was nearing eighty but with a childlike innocence that captivated all who drew near.

"Honey, is Trent still here?" I could count on one hand the times in my life that I heard my parents call each other by their given names, Roger and Alice. I never looked, but I'm sure that neither possessed a birth certificate stating, Honey, as a legal name but it had always been Honey this and Honey that, even during the rare times when they were angry at each other.

I rose quickly. He was leaning on the doorframe to the bathroom. He was a tall man and when I was little, I thought that he was gigantic. Now he was frail and skinny. He had steadfastly refused a walker or any aid that might portray him as weak. He had many shortcomings, but he had enough pride for a dozen men. When his self-importance was challenged as I have done so on many occasions, he retaliated by pointing out my mistakes, and he would not refrain from using ridicule as a tool to ensure that he got the upper hand in a disagreement, especially if there were others present.

"Can you help me get back to the chair?" he asked, struggling for breath.

"Sure, Pop," I replied. "Just take it easy."

I steadied him as I placed one hand where biceps and triceps once existed and the other on his upper back. He wanted to rush to the chair. I knew it was partly because he had always been in a hurry to get from point A to point B, but it was more so now because he feared falling. He was eighty-four, and his life was now reduced to worrying about whether he could negotiate the nine steps remaining to his recliner.

"Pop, don't rush. Take your time. I've got you."

He paused at the doorway. It was now down to five steps. For him, I'm sure it seemed as if it might be a mile away. "Don't rush," I repeated.

Moments later, he was in his chair. "Thank you." His manners seem to have improved with the deterioration of his health.

"You're welcome."

He looked at Mom, his bride of nearly sixty years. "Trent doesn't rush me the way you do."

Mom offered a misplaced smile on a face that was consumed with fatigue. She was wearing down as his primary caretaker.

My parents had always enjoyed a good marriage. They were in love every day since he charmed my mother when she was only twenty years old with his blonde curly hair, which faded away long ago and his gift of gab. She was spoken for by another man when he discovered her. He informed her mother that her daughter would never marry that man. He was right. Confidence was something that the old man never lacked. "I was full of piss and vinegar back then," I have heard him state on occasion. I've yet to completely understand exactly what that statement means, but it was one of the many quotes that I have heard him liberally dispense. I thought it was exclusively his phrase until I heard Paul Newman say it once in a movie. Dad had a plethora of these sayings, and some probably made sense only to him. I never could quite grasp what he meant when he would say, "Jesus, God, I reckon." That was a saying he used when someone chose to do something he just didn't understand. He said it frequently in my presence for some peculiar reason. I always enjoyed the one he used when he observed someone he did not think very highly of. "He's not worth a damn, riding nor walking." This statement was always followed by a dismissive shake of his head. But my favorite saying from my father was when he would say about someone. "Yes, he has a P.H.D., and he couldn't pour piss out of a boot with the directions on the heel." Now that one I fully comprehended. I hope that Paul Newman didn't steal that one from my old man as well.

As a young boy, I would hear my parents talk for a few minutes before falling asleep. Never could I make out a word of what they were saying, and I did not care too. However, something assured me that it was vital that they do this, and I found solace in their routine. My sisters and I never worried about divorce and not because it was not in vogue back then, but because of the genuine affection that our parents shared for each other.

Pop always believed without question that his wife was the prettiest and the best woman around. He could have taken her to dinner with Kings and Queens, and he would have been persuaded no differently. He had always been prouder of her than anything this life offered.

He was angry when I moved to Georgia. On the occasions that I called, he refused to speak to me. No apologies were offered when I walked into the room to see him yesterday. He was watching his beloved Atlanta Braves, and as usual he informed me of what a sorry job the manager was doing. It was as if I had never left.

He struggled to get comfortable in his recliner. Minutes later, his eyes closed, and he was free from his torment, if only for a few minutes.

He would not fool us this time by recovering. He had defied such thinking many times before, and I longed for him to do so once again. But he was like an automobile engine with 400,000 miles on it. There were not enough worthwhile internal components left to repair.

His eyes opened, and he blinked several times as if he was not sure of his surroundings. His distant blue eyes located me. "How was the drive up this morning?"

"It was fine." I don't bother to tell him that I arrived the day before.

He began to speak but stopped. Only impending death could prevent him from talking. The family often said that he would strike up a conversation with the gatepost if there was no one else to tell stories to. He did indeed love to talk. I only wish that he had been able to listen occasionally.

I stood and prepared to depart. I did not tell him that I loved him, and to be candid I often deliberated if either of us truly loved each other. I also chose not to tell him that I loved him because it would make him uncomfortable. He was ill at ease enough with his declining condition. The dignity and pride, which he had clung so fiercely to his entire life, I would not interfere with.

Mom walked out with me. We stopped at the porch, and I knew she wanted to sit and chat. I did so without being asked. The distance between Pop and me had always been more than compensated by the bond shared between my mother and me.

The afternoon was warm, and the sun filtered through the gigantic pine trees, making a partial appearance on the porch. The sparse lawn was ragged with pine straw, fallen limbs, and dogwood leaves. Yard maintenance never was much of a priority for either of them, and they were too frugal to pay someone. At one time, the kids took care of the yard, though I got out of the raking of any pine straw as it would put me in a severe asthma attack each time that I attempted it. The only thing my childhood asthma ever proved good for.

"There is no telling how long he will be this way. I don't want you to lose your job."

"It's okay, Mom." I paused before asking, "You don't think that he will get better this time, do you?"

She dropped her head slightly and forced a smile cloaked in sadness. "He has lost nearly thirty pounds since Christmas. It's more than his heart. Linda wants to put him in another hospital and get him a new doctor."

I listened but there was nothing I had to offer.

"Are you staying with Jackson tonight?"

I nodded my answer.

Jackson sold boats for a living. He also helped me find my current job. It was a simple job, and my limited knowledge of boats had not yet proven to be a detriment.

"It's good to have you home." She paused before continuing, "Well, at least I get to see you when one of the girls takes me shopping to Myrtle Beach, and you meet us there."

"I never meant to hurt you, Mom. I was tired, and I needed to view things in a different light."

"You mean that you ran away from all your failures," she answered swiftly.

"Maybe," I replied evenly, refusing to be baited into a conversation that had been played out far too many times.

Her voice was tender when she asked. "Has it helped?"

"Yes."

She smiled warmly and shifted gears as quickly as a five-year-old child in a candy store. "Have you been to see any of your sisters?"

I looked at her without expression.

"You hurt them by never coming around and even refusing to give us your phone number. Not even to me, your mother. You haven't been back once since you left, not even for Christmas."

"Maybe they should have refrained from always pointing out my errors. I see my missteps clearer than they ever will, and I do call you. I just choose to call from another number because if they ask you for my number, you would crack as quickly as a criminal terrified of prison."

"I never saw them treat you that way."

"You never looked."

"They love you, and they say your childhood with your father was nothing like you recollect."

"How would they know? They are fifteen and seventeen years older than me. All of them were out of this house and married before I was nine years old.

"And how often did they intrude into my life without an invitation? And if I uttered a rebuttal, then I was the bad guy. But all because they love me, right? It's like an escape clause at the end of a contract. Isn't it funny how we butcher each other in the name of love?"

She shook her head. "You isolated yourself from all of us, from everything that you have ever known. You were just years away from retiring from your job. You walked away from a full pension at fifty and health insurance. You could have gotten another job and been better off financially."

"It was the only way. I was dying inside, and I had nothing to lose."

Her voice rose with frustration. "You left because of a woman. After Carmen was gone, you found love again, and when that one failed, you just quit on life."

"I did need to escape, and if I had it to do it all over again, I would. I'm sorry that it hurts you but if nothing else, you know you could always count on my honesty. Even if it was not what you desired."

She eyed me curiously, wondering what was coming next and probably not wanting to hear it. "Mom, you always pretended that things in our family were better than they really were. I know it's what you coveted, just like you always desired for Dad and me to be close."

"He would do anything for you."

"That is mostly true, except for the part where he could have tried listening occasionally and not believing that he always knew what was best in every possible scenario. If you never take the time to learn who someone is, how can you properly advise them?"

She lacked an answer for that one. Several moments passed before she returned to the subject of women. "You dated so many girls that were nice and would have done anything for you."

"I fell in love with the wrong women. Twice. Believe me. I know that."

Tiring of the conversation, I rose to leave. "I'm going now." I kissed her goodbye.

"What about your son? Are you going to see him? You gave him all the things that you claim that you never received from your father and yet you abandoned him."

"I hurt him, Mom."

"He forgave you. He always did."

I opened the screen door and walked away calmly.

"It's a shame you couldn't forgive yourself. But then you never could. Always too damn busy dragging yesterday around to see what's in front of you today." The wooden door closed harshly behind her last words.

I drove through the neighborhood that, as a child, was made up of mostly dirt roads. Mom's last words still rang in my ears. Seldom does she get upset, and even less often does she offer even a mild profanity.

The time seemed longer than thirty plus years since I played on and around these same streets. Sports were an everyday part of our youth. We played baseball, football, basketball, and my favorite, stickball, with my friend Rick. We played for hours in the hot sun on the dead-end street in front of his home. His brother, Al, joined on occasion.

Memories drifted to homemade putt-putt courses-the big tree-the big ditch-the hills that were merely dirt dug from the big ditch.

I ventured down a seldom-used road that runs behind Rick and Al's childhood home. I paused to observe the modest brick home where their dad now lives alone. Their mom passed away many years ago. He was successful in business and could have long ago departed from our modest neighborhood in Sea Gate, but he never desired to leave for a bigger house. They had the only cement basketball court in the neighborhood, which was shared liberally. I played hundreds of games on that small court that was bordered on three sides by tall pine trees. There was never a place I enjoyed playing the beautiful game of basketball more than here with the boys of my youth. Fights with ugly words often broke out but by the next day, it was as if nothing ruinous had ever transpired.

There was a weathered bench by the court where we sat and savored the refreshments purchased from a little store within walking distance. That old wooden store was long gone, replaced by yet another strip mall.

Off to my right, I looked through the trees and caught a glimpse of the old baseball diamond that we played pickup games on. The field was constructed during a time when Semi-pro baseball was as much a part of Sundays in the summertime as attending church.

I parked my car on the side of the road and walked through the trail that had narrowed considerably without the steady traffic of children. At the end of the trail, the field abruptly opened. The grass in the outfield was two feet tall, and the grass in the skin infield was so thick that the clay was barely visible. For as long as I could recall, I always felt a disturbing sadness, a barren sentiment, when viewing an empty baseball field in winter. That same emotion is present as I stared out at the decaying field. A sign in centerfield declared that the land had been sold and that condominiums could be purchased at pre-construction prices.

Baseball was once our national pastime but now it's perceived as being too slow. I was guilty of this viewpoint as well, but I speculated as to if it was actually that baseball became too slow or was it the speed of our own lives that have aborted our love affair of the grand game?

I returned to my car, and as I entered the main highway, I pressed the pedal down hard. My only real possession, the black Z that I bought to escape town hugs the road. I turned up the volume to Guns and Roses singing "Sweet Child of Mine" in hopes that it would drown out the clatter in my head. It failed to do so once again.

4

Various boats passed by as I stood on the dock outside of the small business where Jackson worked. He was showing a boat to another person of affluence. The price of these boats demanded wealth. He had struggled for years to make his way in a business that necessitated extreme perseverance.

I met him several years ago at a small dingy fitness club in Wrightsville Beach. Many of my friendships had dwindled through the years, but ours had grown. There was a good reason that he was the only person that knew my exact whereabouts. If you told him something, it stayed in the vault, where it would be locked away forever.

I gazed across the waterway toward Wrightsville Beach. To each side of me, the Intracoastal Waterway stretched as far as the eye could see. The nuisance drawbridge that should have been put out of its misery long before it became fashionably quaint temporarily obstructed the view to my left.

I turned and walked inside. The lobby area contained three garish nautical themed couches and a glass table that held a multitude of boat and fishing magazines. Across from that area was an oval shaped teak wood countertop. There was a chair behind it where the administrative assistant sat when she was working. I entered a small room that contained a refrigerator, sink, microwave, and a small wooden table. I opened the fridge and discovered that my friend had it stocked for clients. There were cans of Miller Lite and bottles of Corona. Easy choice. The cold sweat on the outside of the bottle felt good against my hand. On the table rested a basket of limes. I grabbed one and checked the drawer, locating an opener and a sharp knife. I opened the beer, sliced a piece of lime, and squeezed it lightly into the bottle.

There was a restaurant next door. Two men strummed guitars on the dock. One of them sang "Take it Easy" by the Eagles. A small crowd enjoyed adult beverages. A large sailboat glided smoothly to the pier. It was moored quickly by two men. A glamorous looking couple stepped from the boat onto the dock. I recognized the woman instantly. Shannon.

We shared an incredible night a few years ago in a Park on a stormy night. But she was married, and it was also during the fringe of the time that Carmen and I fell in love for the second time, many years apart. We were convinced that this time we would not prove too young to grasp the treasure we had in our depth of feeling for each other.

Carmen invaded my thoughts several times daily. Occasionally, I allowed myself to consider that if I would have granted her request on the last night of her life that she would be with me today. But by that point, she had dissipated any hope or trust I once held for her.

Shannon finally left an unhappy marriage, something I never thought she would do. She wore an aqua wrap around her waist. The sun bounced off of her generous cleavage that was barely contained in her matching aqua bikini top. Suddenly she turned and her eyes locked on me. I raised my beer in a slight toast, and she turned quickly back to her new husband without acknowledgment. He wore tan pants and a long sleeve white linen shirt. His hair was silvery gray and full. He reminded me of Ted Knight in the movie *Caddyshack.*

Maybe if we had been free and clear, she would have proven the right woman. But she had a husband and children, and I had to venture down a path that was marked only for me. I made the choices and suffered the blows. I chuckled as I heard Frank Sinatra singing in my head. I faced it all, and I stood tall and did it my way. No risk, no reward was how I had lived life for so long. I mocked those who were afraid to chance.

Drinking heartily from my beer, I was reminded that I lived alone, and my heart was as fastened shut as the people I once disparaged. There was nothing quite so chastening as coming to grips with your own hypocrisy.

The theme of separation continued in my reflections and I thought of Alex and the last time I saw her. It was a late summer day on the beach.

Her last statements she offered were, "I am on the upscale of my career, and you are on the downside. You have lived here your entire life, and you will never leave. I want to travel the world. We are just too different."

This same woman once shared that she had not always known what was truly important, but she was grasping more and more of what was indeed of significance each day that she spent with me. Fast forward to the end, and I was merely a man without the drive for success and financial means that she deemed essential.

I could still see her standing–clad in that orange bikini. Straight black hair falling until it touched her shoulders. The dark, almost black eyes that could harden and soften with the quickness of a rattlesnake strike and always carried a hint of sorrow if you discerned judiciously. Prominent cheekbones. Skin so tan that it reminded me of an early night. A body toned in every place.

I sat outside and observed the Bertram 61 ease carefully beside the dock. Two teenage boys grabbed the lines and tied the boat down. Jackson was talking with the prospective buyer, who was dressed in a soft gray linen suit. Not a strand of his white hair was out of place. He carried the image of wealth, and looking at a $3.5-million boat was merely part of the day. He walked briskly by as if I failed to exist. Jackson nodded in my direction and walked the man to his silver Mercedes convertible.

Jackson stopped in his office and returned with two beers. He gave one to me and sat in the chair next to me. He was dressed in khaki pants and a hunter green polo shirt. Our friendship did not have to be disturbed by words. The sun sat atop of the trees in the distance.

"How long can you put me up?"

He shrugged as if my question was not worth an answer before offering, "Until one of us gets married."

I smiled. "You got plans?"

He feigned a glare at me. "I've made it almost four decades without a wife. I think I will stick to what works."

Moments passed before he asked, "How's your dad?"

"Dying," I answered before adding, "Jackson, don't advertise that I am here. I left, and I don't want to explain to anyone why."

"I pretty much had a handle on that," he said dryly. "But one day I would like for you to tell me why."

"Don't you know?"

"I know it was more than a breakup with Alex."

I looked at him and remained silent. He nodded, understanding that now was not the time for clarification.

We watched the sun disappear behind the trees. Birds flew in the last shimmering lights that danced upon the water. Off to the north, a thunderhead appeared and steadily moved in our direction. In the distance, heat lightning flashed and a sudden breeze emerged, and the air cooled.

"Let's go home," he said. "Ride with me. I'll bring you back in the morning." He had noticed the six empty bottles by my chair.

"Better yet, why don't you drive the Z," I responded, tossing him the keys.

5

The first light of morning offered a view of the creeks and marsh grass that extended infinitely. I looked east in the direction of the ocean. The blue sky was painted with traces of pink, orange and red. Directly in front, a fish jumped. Jackson would, in that fleeting moment, probably know what type of fish it was. I was reminded of an old worship song. Most of the words eluded me now but the chorus line dealt with the majesty of God. That was what I viewed at the moment.

Jackson lived in the house that his parents built long ago on the island of Wrightsville Beach. It was back in an era, long departed, when middle class folks could afford to purchase a home here.

His mom died suddenly a few years ago, and his dad remarried a few years later. He and his wife lived in a town just outside of Wilmington.

The house was modest. The cedar exterior had long ago weathered to a dark shade of gray. There was one floor of living area that rested on pilings. A garage was located underneath, but I never saw a car parked there. There was, however, a twenty-four foot sail boat that his dad began building many years ago. It sat collecting dust with tools resting comfortably inside of it.

I sat down on the deck and slipped a pair of weathered running shoes on. I began an assortment of stretching exercises that have become more pertinent with age. Minutes later, I was jogging on the popular loop.

Off to my left was the park, where I worked for over twenty years. Mom was right. I was so close to early retirement, but I knew that I had to leave. The job, as well as my life here, was killing me.

No one could understand, least of all my family. There was pain in my father right now that was clearly visible. I found that it was the concealed hurt that cuts the deepest, but people couldn't picture it easily because it did not prove tangible. It was easier for them to analyze and criticize the person for not being able to wave a magic wand and make the illness disappear. With age and experiencing the sorrow that life could bring, I had learned to be less critical of what I could not see or understand.

Though the temperature dipped into the fifties, I was perspiring within minutes. There was pain in my left knee. The one that was not operated on. I probably should avoid running, and stick to lifting weights and riding the bike in the gym. I loved lifting weights, but there was nothing like a run to clear my mind.

Thinking of my knee surgery took my mind unwillingly back to Alex. It was when my son, Brooks, and I had just moved in with her, yet another of my foolish decisions.

***

It was not yet six a.m. on an early summer morning. Alex talked easily as she drove me to the hospital in her new ride, a dark green BMW sports car. She purchased this vehicle for many reasons, but the main one was the horsepower that it possessed. The girl became as giddy discussing horsepower as a Nascar race driver. I can't describe how beautiful she looked, her black hair flowing in the wind as we rode with the top down.

I attempted to talk her out of driving me but she insisted. She dropped me off outside the entrance, kissed me and told me that she would be home at eight that night. She drove away to a management firm where she was already a vice president at the age of thirty-two.

Mom arrived a few minutes later and sat with me until the drugs kicked in, and a team rolled me to the surgical room. She walked to the lobby, sat and read from her worn Bible. Later, I discovered that Alex had returned. After an hour of talking with mom, she sent her away to her weekly prayer meeting.

It was after the surgery, and I was in the recovery room. Alex walked in. She wore a sharp black business dress.

"But—"

"Hush," she said as she kissed me.

She drove us home and helped me negotiate the steps that led to her condo. She helped me to the couch and fluffed a pillow for me. She walked to the kitchen and returned with a Diet Sun-Drop and placed it on the table beside me. A table nearly covered with an assortment of candles. I liked candles. She adored them. She bent to kiss me and placed the television remote on my chest. "Comfy on my ugly couch?"

The couch was oversized and outdated with a checkered design of black and white. It was, indeed, unattractive. I loved it. She spoke of getting rid of it, but I requested she not do so. We had memories on this couch.

"When we get a house together, we will put it in your playroom, where I will banish you to when you insist on watching sports."

She kissed me goodbye and turned to depart. She was almost to the door when she spun back. It was like all her movements. Quick, efficient, and unrehearsed. "Quite the conversation that I had with your mother. She talked about how good you are to her, and then she said, 'they say when a son is good to his mother; he will make a good husband.' I think she hopes that I am the one. That's what I hope for as well." She departed, leaving me with warmth that can't be described.

It was past eight when she returned. An accomplished marathoner, she probably ran ten miles after work. She ran Chicago in 3:30 and San Diego, her hometown, in 3:18. I was in the Jacuzzi with my knee out of the water. I heard the shower running in the other bathroom.

Minutes later, she appeared in a nurse uniform, complete with cap. For weeks I teased her about buying a nurse outfit, and each time she offered a look of complete indifference. It was difficult for her to give of herself, and I knew that when I embarked down this path.

"How is the patient?" she inquired.

"Fine, no pain."

"Would you say so if it did hurt?"

"No, but it really doesn't."

I stepped out of the tub, and she dried me off. "Follow me," she said.

She led me to her bedroom. Later, as we lay together peacefully, I said, "Wow, you are some nurse."

She rose over me and reached across the bed for her nurse's cap. She put it on and said cheerfully, "Well, I came home and found the patient in the Jacuzzi in good spirits and took care of his needs as well as my own."

***

I was into mile five now, and I ran harder in an attempt to shake her from my mind. We were together for less than a year, but my trepidations were that she might rent storage in my head indefinitely. I always thought it would have been great if God would have created us with a valve on our head like the one on a basketball. Each year, on a designated day, we would be allowed to deflate all the bad memories that haunted us.

Daily Carmen and Alex frequented my thoughts. I feared that it would always be that way. Alex once said that I had a huge heart and a mind that never stilled. Sadly, she was correct. I have known so very little peace in my life, and when those fleeting moments of tranquility appeared, I knew that they were not to be trusted.

I ended my run, left the sidewalk, and walked through Harbor Way Gardens. Many years ago, I planted trees and countless daylilies on these grounds. The ladies of the

Harbor Island Garden Club took charge of the area many years ago and had transformed it into a beautiful lush garden.

At the back of the garden, a lady nearing seventy but with the work ethic of someone much younger was spreading mulch. I knew her and thought that I might just be able to keep walking and avoid conversation. Maybe she wouldn't see me.

I managed a few steps before I heard her stern voice. I felt like a school kid caught skipping class.

"Trent Mullins. Do not attempt to walk by like you don't see me."

I turned and forced a smile. "Linda."

Linda was perceived by many as being tough as nails but I have been blessed to know the tender parts of her.

"I am not going to fuss at you for leaving."

I nodded my appreciation.

"I miss you."

I smiled in response.

We chatted for a few minutes before she informed me she needed to return to work. We exchanged goodbyes and I walked away.

"I love you, Trent Mullins."

I turned back and smiled broadly. "I love you too, sweetheart."

I smelled coffee as I neared the steps. I removed my wet tee shirt and walked up the steps. Jackson was sitting on the deck, a mug the color of dark chocolate in his hand. He looked at me, and his eyes narrowed with surprise.

"What?"

"Dang, your stomach is flat."

"You know those beers last night were the first alcohol I tasted since I left here."

"You're kidding."

"Swear to you."

"And I've eaten better for the most part," as I thought about the meals served by Moses and Maybelle. "I have a Weber Grill, and I cook chicken breasts and broccoli or asparagus almost every night."

His face squinted with a look of bewilderment. He knew of my love for a cold beer at the end of the day. It was a love that he shared as well. "Why would you go so long without a beer?"

"I was so depressed when I left. I thought that it would be better to abstain. My intentions were that it would be for a little while, but I just kept away from it. That is until I returned here to sin city and got around you."

He sipped his coffee and eyed me warily over the rim of the mug. "Yeah, blame your mess on me. I see how you are."

"You don't expect me to blame myself, do you?"

"Yes," he stated evenly. "Just like always. Even for stuff that wasn't your fault."

He looked out at the water and paused before speaking. "It was probably a good idea not to drink. Besides, it's not really the breakup with a woman that pains you so badly. It's the alcohol that you need to consume to forget them."

He cackled with amusement at his statement. His hand darted up, and he deftly brushed his light brown hair from his forehead. He had a boyish face and the only concession to age was the slight crow's feet outside his eyes.

His laughter subsided, and his smile faded. "Do you still blame yourself for everything?"

"Pretty much."

"You just made some poor choices. We all do. You need to let things go."

I opened the sliding glass door and walked to the kitchen, and retrieved a bottle of mineral water from the fridge. I searched the cabinets for two storage bags. Finding them, I opened the freezer door and gathered ice, filling each bag. I returned to the deck, sat, and propped both legs on a short wooden bench. I placed a bag of ice on each knee. "When did you get so philosophical so early in the morning?"

"Are you still depressed?"

"No."

His eyes narrowed. "Are you happy?"

"That would be a stretch."

He rotated his shoulders in each direction, trying to loosen the stiffness in his back. He sipped his coffee and returned it to the railing. "When you absconded from here, I was certain you would be back inside of six months."

He gathered his mug again and held it with both hands. "What I don't understand is why you couldn't come back at all. Until now, that is."

I offered no explanation.

He looked out into the water as if he were searching for something that would help him eloquently convey what was on his mind. He was always slow to make conclusions. If you had a problem, he was good to talk to because you got his undivided attention and a sincere willingness to help. You had just better not expect an answer this month.

"I love you, and the island isn't the same without you."

It was unlike him to offer such words, and they stung me quickly with their sentiment. My eyes welled without warning. I rose from the chair and walked a few steps away, pretending to search for another view of the water.

I didn't hear him as he approached. His hand clasped my shoulder firmly. "I mean it," he said.

I turned, and it disconcerted me to see the water in my friend's eyes.

6

I showered and minutes later, we walked down the street to a nearby restaurant. The business was a gold mine. It was one of the few places on the island that turned a profit in the winter when the area was inhabited by year-round residents, and the tourists were still months away from their annual invasion. They served lunch, but breakfast had always proven the busiest time of the day. We walked inside and were immediately immersed in the aroma of sausage, bacon, eggs, grits, hash browns, and biscuits that a southern restaurant so charitably offered.

We sat in a booth. The brown Formica table had not been updated in twenty years. There was no need. No one came here for the interior decor.

A short, overweight waitress with shoulder-length honey-blonde hair approached our table with pad and pen in hand, offering no words. Jackson ordered coffee, and I asked if they had Diet Sun-Drop. She nodded and returned moments later with Jackson's coffee and my soft drink. She took our food orders, still without offering a word.

"Since you have been abstaining from alcohol, I bet you drink about ten of those a day," he said, gesturing at my glass of yellow liquid.

"One. Then it's water for the rest of the day."

"What a boring life."

I smiled and replied, "Yeah, but the Diet Sun Drop gives me a reason to wake up in the morning."

"Do you need a reason to wake up each morning?"

Scratching my head slightly, I said, "You ask a lot of questions."

Nodding slightly, he turned his attention toward the waitress who arrived at our table with plates of food. Our breakfast contained omelets filled with crabmeat and cheese, along with hash browns and biscuits. Jackson began to eat. I deliberated if I had hurt his feelings. I would be surprised because he was not sensitive about things, and his feelings certainly don't bruise easily as mine do. Alex once labeled me hypersensitive. I disliked it at the time. Primarily because I knew that she was correct.

Maybe that was why she said the things she did in the end. Because she knew that regardless of how unjustified her words were that they would still enter and tear at me repetitively. I knew that what she said was wrong and hypocritical.

Jackson paused from eating. He looked at my plate, which was untouched. "Are you going to eat?" He continued to study me. "Look, I'm not being nosy. You have always been such an open book. There was a time that I couldn't shut you up. Talking about love, your hopes, and dreams. Your book would be a big hit, and I was going on the book tour with you. Now you're closed off from dreams, your family, your friends."

After my split with Carmen, I passed the time by writing. I wrote a fictional story about two young men, one black and one white, who became friends during a racially charged time when friends of different races did not exactly hang out together. I finished it, and I was excited, right up until about the twentieth rejection.

"I didn't close off from you."

"It's not the same. We can't pick up the phone and meet for dinner. I see you when I run a boat up from Florida and stop by your work."

"I thought at times that I asked too much from you."

"Aw, the hell with that!" He spoke louder than he likely intended. A man in the next booth, with his wife and two small children, glared at him.

Jackson held both hands out, his palms facing downward. "I'm sorry," he said to the man. The man nodded lightly and instantly withdrew his harsh judgmental look. We ate in silence for the rest of the meal.

The sun was higher now, and the wind moved gently as we meandered back to his place. There was an uncomfortable hush as we walked. Uncomfortable was not a word that I thought that I would ever use concerning the two of us.

We sat in two old wicker rocking chairs, and as always, viewed the marshlands. A pelican swooped down in a creek and came away with a small fish. In another creek, a small aluminum boat headed toward the waterway. A man tossed his hand up toward us as his black lab wrestled for purchase on the bow. We waved in return.

"I didn't mean anything back there."

"I know," he replied softly. He continued, "Why would you ever think that I had done more for you than you have for me?"

"Because I needed more."

He shook his head slightly. "When my mother died, was there ever a time that I needed anything and you were not there? It wouldn't matter if you did need more. Friends never keep score. You know that. So, you didn't think that I would see you through a second heartbreak? I'd be there for you if it happened a dozen times."

"I know that."

"I have always admired the way you hang your heart out in the wind for all to see. I struggle to do that. It seems that you are not that way anymore, and I think that it is a waste." He turned to me, and his face is as severe as I have ever witnessed it. "You are a person of heart. It is who you will always be regardless of your attempt to live otherwise." He paused, and there was quiet for a few moments. I observed a wry smile emerge from him. "I read the book that you wrote," he said.

Now, this was indeed a revelation. I have never known him to read anything beyond an article in fishing or boating magazines. "It's only a book if a publisher publishes it. What you read was words on paper. A manuscript. And how did you even get your hands on it to read it, if indeed you did?"

"I asked your mom if she had a copy."

"You read the entire thing? How long did it take you? A year?"

"One week."

"Right," I answered sarcastically.

"One week," he repeated, before adding, "It was good."

"Too bad no publisher agreed. Oh, I got some nice compliments. An ambitious piece of work with good intent. It moved me, but the writing is not strong enough."

"Write another one."

"Why?"

His voice rose in anger for the second time this morning. "Do you know what a gift it is to draw a story out of your heart like that? Some of us are not passionate about anything."

"Hey, I've seen you fish before," I said, chuckling, in an attempt to lighten the mood.

He failed to laugh with me. He gazed out toward the water, observing another boat pass by. "Watching you believe in the things that actually matter always made me feel good about this life. Sometimes, I even thought I could throw caution to the wind and sail away with the right woman. Now you have become too much like me."

I was amazed to hear my best friend say these things. "Jackson, I don't know what to say."

"You just have to turn the page again. You know, like the song by Bob Dylan."

I loved music from the sixties till today. I had never heard Jackson talk about music. His lack of knowledge showed at the moment.

"Bob Seger, you idiot."

Looking perplexed, he said, "What?"

"Bob Seger wrote, "Turn the Page." Not Bob Dylan."

"Oh," he replied, completely unoffended.

A comfortable hush surfaced for several minutes before he softly inquired, "Why did you feel like you had to disappear? And please don't tell me it was about Alex. As I recall, you were having anxiety problems wondering what type of mood she would be in when she came home. I thought you were actually relieved when it ended. You were the one who said, let's end it now."

I failed to answer.

"I ran into her friend, Norma, soon after you left. She said that Alex had made a lot of changes. Searching for a more meaningful way of life and that she had changed, but not enough to commit to a man like you."

"Yeah, a man like me."

"Hey," he said, raising his voice. "She meant it as a compliment. There is nobody I know who knows what is truly important in this life more than you. Alex fell in love with you. She left a world that she was comfortable in to be uncomfortable. Don't you see the good in that?"

"No. Only the pain left in its wake."

Undeterred, he continued, "Eventually, the flashy, beautiful women like her follow the money. I witness it all the time. I know you saw Shannon yesterday. Do you think she loves that old fart she's with?"

"Who knows?"

"It seems to me that you allowed Alex to win. She lost out. Do you think that she will ever find anyone who will love her the way you did? If she ever does open herself to marriage, she will be some pompous guy's trophy wife. She might as well be a stuffed swordfish mounted on the wall."

"Love isn't a contest. Nobody wins when it's over. That is just a senseless game people play. A way to save face when most people don't care."

"I know that. Now, why did you leave? I want an answer this time, a real answer."

"Okay. Alex hurt me badly with some of the things she said in the end. About how content I was to stay in the same place. I didn't have her drive for work or success. I don't have a desire to travel the world."

"You left to prove a point?" His face was covered in exasperation.

"Maybe a little."

"Did you want her back then?"

"You know it hurt, but I knew that I was better off without her. Your head knows this, but your heart has such a hard time letting go. Everywhere you go, there is a reminder."

He gripped my arm firmly. "After you and Carmen split, you finally reached a point where you didn't care. The constant reminders subsided, and these would have as well. But not by running."

I breathed in deeply. "It seemed like all the cumulative pain in my life caught up with me at one time. Forty years of mistakes. That was all I could see. The pain outweighed anything else. It was greater than the people I loved. It was greater than my home. I knew that I couldn't run from my problems, but I did think that it might help to look at them from another vantage point." Sighing, I added, "Things happen for a reason. Isn't that the old saying?"

I knew that my friend was searching for words that would implore me to move back home, but all I could think of was how badly I wanted to depart for the solitude of the marshlands of Georgia.

"Don't Let the Sun Go Down on Me" began to play. I answered and received directions from my sister, Lydia. "Family meeting, five o'clock today at her house. Be nice if you could make it." Sarcasm heavily interjected into every word. I don't think she even said bye.

I ended the call and responded tersely, "I am changing my number when I return to Georgia."

The look in my friend's eyes informed me that was not the response he desired.

7

Family meeting scheduled in one hour. I could scarcely wait. I was not invited so that they could hear my opinions on the matters at hand. Not that I could blame them. I was the one that left.

All of my well-educated sisters had proven very successful in their careers and lives. Connie and her husband were the most prosperous if you are keeping score, and there is always a tally to be kept in our family. They lived in Greensboro for the past four years, after several business ventures in various places. All of their professional endeavors had proven successful but they now owned a company that recycled plastics. Last year they were featured in an article in the *Wall Street Journal*. Their wealth was somewhere in the neighborhood of fifty million dollars. While not amassing that kind of fortune, my remaining sisters and their husbands were probably worth five million dollars. They were also all still married to their high school or college sweethearts, and along the way, they managed to do the American thing and have two point five children. Today they enjoyed the fruits of grandchildren.

As for me, I barely made it out of high school. I began drinking and smoking marijuana when I was thirteen. At age eighteen I was convicted for throwing a chair through a restaurant window because the owner said something ingenious about my date being a few shades darker than me. Here we were on the fringe of the Deep South, so I bet you were assuming that it had to be another good old confederate flag waving redneck. You would be in error. This guy was from New York City.

I understand the history and the racism that still existed in the South. I had no tolerance for any of it, but please let's don't act like bigotry only occurs in the South. I had heard many transplanted northerners boldly declare interracial dating wrong. They were just as prejudiced in much of their thinking. They just don't wave confederate flags.

Did I mention that I was the only one in the family to be divorced? You decide. I was either the reprobate of the family or a trendsetter.

It was time to go. I dressed in blue jeans, a long-sleeve black tee-shirt, and a pair of black with blue trim Under Armour, Steph Curry sneakers. I retrieved my limited cash from the top of the dresser reminding me that I needed funds to live on while I was here. I left Georgia hurriedly and mistakenly without my ATM card or even a credit card. Howard would be back in two weeks, and I told him before he departed for his vacation not to worry about paying me my monthly wage until he returned from Greece. Well, maybe Mom hadn't completely disowned me.

I walked outside to my car, fired the engine up, and backed out of the drive. Never in my life had I owned a sports car.

A running buddy, Josh, once suggested that Alex dated rich flashy guys who drove sports cars and that I was batting zero in those three categories.

Before we began our torrid relationship, I thought she was stuck on her beauty, which lent her a reason to be cold towards people. Later, when I discovered a softer side, I found that what she was hiding behind was not her exquisite looks but rather her plethora of insecurities. She would laugh when I told her how wonderful she looked. It reached the point where I would hold her mouth with my hand gently and say, "God, you look beautiful tonight." It didn't work. She would laugh into my hand. There was so much hidden away inside of her that I wanted to explore, but she closed off when it reached beyond a level of ease that she could comfortably live with.

Josh's words echoed in my head, and I have to admit that everyone she dated that I knew of matched the description that he offered with the obvious exception of me. Who knows what I was thinking when I bought this car? Everything was muddied. Maybe it was as simple as having something fun in my life when there was so little to be found, or perhaps it was purchasing something with charged horsepower to escape the town I once so treasured as expeditiously as possible.

Mom sat on the porch as I entered the drive. I shut the engine off, walked up the brick steps, and sat across from her.

"I'm sorry about yesterday," she said.

"Don't worry about it."

She blinked her eyes before tears emerged. Wiping her cheeks, she continued, "I just didn't want to see you go."

"I know." I don't want a repeat of yesterday. I rose and said gently, "I'm going in to see Dad."

He was asleep in his recliner. I sat across from him on the couch. For some reason, I recalled the day he interrupted a pickup basketball game and chased me around the neighborhood with his wide black belt. He was like a madman. He also could not catch a terrified fourteen-year-old kid.

I could still see him standing in the neighbor's driveway, holding that belt and waving it menacingly. "You might as well come here."

I shook my head and when he charged, I sprinted away. His bad knee buckled inside of ten yards, and he relinquished pursuit. My friends stood motionless. Eyes gaped in fear.

My reaction was to return home and pack some clothes. He was in the yard when I walked around him at a safe distance. It wasn't necessary because he was too tired to continue his mission to beat the hell out of me. I'll never forget the perplexed look on his face when he noticed my sleeping bag. For once, he was rendered speechless. One week later, I returned home, and no mention was ever made of that day. And he never thought about bringing a belt around his teenage son again.

As I reflected on this incident, I felt sympathy for him as I often do. It was yet another thing he did recklessly that he saw no need to be ashamed of. If not for me, couldn't he have at least contemplated the fear he invoked in those kids that witnessed his crazed lunacy? I know the answer to my rhetorical question. It never crossed his mind.

I heard Mom in their bedroom. I walked to the doorway and smiled. "Since you have decided that you still love me, I need a favor."

"What is it?"

"I forgot my ATM card."

"I'll write you a check," she said, moving toward her purse. "How much do you need?"

"Can you do $400.00?"

I know the answer to the question. They were not rich, but they had spent a lifetime storing up for The Next Great Depression. I've joked often with them that it will be a shame if they don't get the opportunity to live through one since they have spent most of their lives preparing for it.

"Get it from up there."

Surprised, I turned back to the origin of the voice. Dad motioned to his hiding place. "Go ahead," he said as he gestured with his hand once again.

Now he had often loaned me money and just as often, I have paid him back. But he liked to be paid back quickly.

"I'll get it from Mom."

"No," he said, trying to muster enough strength to be stern. "Get it from up there," he repeated as he pointed to the top of the cheap particle board entertainment center.

"It might be a couple of weeks before I can pay you back."

"That's okay."

I felt Mom tug on my elbow. I turned to her, and she gestured for me to take the money.

"Thanks, Pop, "I said as I counted off four one-hundred-dollar bills.

"You always pay me back. My wife, I can't say the same for."

"Honey," Mom said sternly, feigning anger.

"How much is left, Trent?" he asked.

Counting the remainder, I said, "$950.00."

"When are you going to pay me the fifty you got last week?" he inquired of her before closing his eyes.

Despite all of his trips to the emergency room, many of which he couldn't recall the details of, he always knew the correct amount of his funds. He smiled briefly. Part of it was his joke on her, but I thought even more so it was that he felt useful once again.

"Thanks for the loan, Pop." His eyes remained closed, and he lifted his right hand slowly, waving it gently like a floating leaf in a lazy wind. I said goodbye and walked in the direction of my car for my engagement with my sisters.

I deliberated about skipping the meeting. I looked around at a back yard that was matted with straw, broken limbs and pinecones. Machinery parts, plumbing, electrical, lawn mowers, and God only knows what was scattered around an old green shed that stood awkwardly by the edge of the woods. The old man never discarded anything. Some of these things had lain around for twenty years, but he still thought that there might be a use for them one day. He would change spark plugs and throw the old ones in his toolbox. This was another area that I learned in reverse from him. I hoarded nothing, and I refused to keep anything that might be of use at some point in the next decade.

Minutes later, I drove through the wealthy, gated community. I hoped the guard would not allow me to pass, but she was cute, blonde, and had an endearing smile. She would probably have allowed a known fugitive access.

I walked the path of brick pavers that lead to a door that probably cost more than I make in a month. Reluctantly, I rang the bell.

"Come in," I heard at least two people say.

I entered the house, which was open and inviting. I don't expect to receive the same from the people inside. Connie got off the first shot. Mockingly she clapped her hands slowly and steadily. The others joined her. "Well, the prodigal son has returned. Aren't we the lucky ones?"

My expression was blank.

Chloe was next. She waited with pen and paper. "Let me have your cell phone number. If Daddy dies, I won't have to go through Jackson first." She turned to her sisters. "You know Jackson is more important than we are."

I gave her my number and I was tempted to agree with her about Jackson but I refrained.

Lydia was next. "So, did running away solve all of your problems?"

"It helped."

"I could have told you that things wouldn't work out with Alex. My friend, Beth said so from day one."

"Well, I'm certain that Beth and you derive much comfort from being correct."

"Champagne tastes on a beer budget," Linda added.

I felt my eyes squint. "And that means?"

"It means little brother, that two women broke your heart. Both of them were beautiful and had way more money than you."

I nodded my understanding, if not my agreement. "As much as I'm enjoying this, I thought this was about Dad."

The room was finally silent.

Linda broke the stillness, and I was relieved that I was no longer the topic of discussion. "I spoke with a doctor yesterday who deals specifically with geriatric patients. If we checked Daddy back into the hospital, she has agreed to be his doctor." She paused before adding, "And he wants to go back to the hospital."

The conversation bounced around for another twenty minutes. I offered nothing. It was decided that an ambulance would be called tomorrow morning and he would be checked into the hospital.

I rose to escape. "We were going to order pizza and eat at Mom and Dad's," Chloe said kindly.

"Sorry, I have other plans."

"Just as well," Connie said.

"Do you grace everyone with that condescending tone?"

"I save it just for you."

"Boy, thanks for the privilege."

"Well, we don't all neglect our families the way you do."

The line had just been drawn in the sand. I was successful at keeping my voice from rising, but the edge to it was hard. "You have not lived in this city in almost forty years. How many times did you get out of bed and meet the EMTs in the middle of the night? I don't think you have the right to say anything to me."

"No, you're wrong, Trent."

I laughed. "I knew that was coming. Never have you said that you were wrong. Not one time in all these years. You just always pull that patronizing tone and say, 'No, it's you who is wrong. It must be such a heavy burden to be so damn perfect."

There was no response this time, and tears formed in her eyes. Once again, I would be the bad guy. "It's been a lot of fun," I said as I headed for the door.

"What did you expect? A royal homecoming?" Chloe asked.

I felt the smile engulf my face. "No, this was exactly what I anticipated." I walked out the door and moved briskly toward my car. Once I was on the highway, I noticed that I was driving over sixty in a forty-five mile per hour zone. I slowed down and breathed deeply. Drawing nearer to the island, I saw the ABC store off to my right. I turned in and parked.

Minutes later, after a quick stop at the grocery store, I headed to Jackson's with a half-gallon of tequila, a pint of premium tequila, margarita mixer, and all the ingredients for taco salad.

Jackson arrived home an hour later. I was cooking and enjoying my fourth margarita.

"How did the meeting go?" he inquired.

I slid a margarita across the counter in his direction and poured a shot of the good stuff on top of it. "Shut up and drink," I said, turning my attention back to cooking.

"That well, eh?" he said as he lifted the glass to his lips.

8

I drifted back in time to the day I decided to move to Georgia. It was a month after the split with Alex. I sat in Jackson's office waiting for him to finish a phone call so we could go to lunch. He ended the call. "Let's go," he said.

We walked out of his office and into the small lobby. We were almost to the door when the phone rang. The administrative assistant had already departed for lunch. The machine picked up the call on the fourth ring. Jackson paused to listen.

"Jackson, Howard. Hey, I was thinking of trading my boat in. You got anything?"

Jackson leaned across the counter and hit the speaker button. "You're full of it."

Howard's laugh roared like an extended clap of rumbling thunder. "How's the boat business?"

"Slow."

"Good."

"Why is that good?" Jackson looked at me and whispered, "This guy is wide-open."

"Jackson, why am I on speakerphone? And who are you telling lies about me to?"

"Don't worry. It's my buddy, Trent. I was telling him what a nice guy you are."

"Yeah, nice guy, my big old butt. Hey, Trent," his voice boomed loudly. "Damn poor taste in friends you got."

"Howard, is there a point to this call?" Jackson asked.

"You know the next time I purchase a boat; I think I will shop around. Maybe buy something besides a Bertram, or find another Bertram dealer."

Jackson played along. "Please don't do that, Mr. Howard. Besides, your wife likes me, and she might get upset."

"I'm glad she likes somebody."

"Might help matters if you steered clear of those Hooter girls."

"Now that is just plain wrong," he said with false indignation. "Now, if you are through busting on me, I would like to get down to business."

"Proceed, sir," Jackson replied with a shake of his head.

"Remember the guy who was heading south last fall, and his boat broke down near you, and you found a guy to do the repair work?"

"I do."

"Well, the boat has been ready for quite some time, and he hasn't found the time to bring it home. He wants to hire you to run it down here for him. "What do you get $400 a day, plus expenses?"

"That's close."

"Close? You think I got this rich by not doing my homework?"

"I thought it was just sheer dumb luck."

Howard laughed loudly. "That's rich, boy. Anyway, I told him that it was $550.00 daily, plus expenses." He paused and then added, "You're sorry you talked disrespectfully to me now, aren't you?"

I could picture this guy sitting back in an expensive leather swivel chair, gold chain around his neck with a cigar the size of a carrot jutting from his mouth.

"When does he want the boat?"

"How about by the end of next week?"

"I can do that. By the way, how is your little venture into the marina business?"

He stammered, coughed, and cursed under his breath. "That is a worse subject right now than my wife's credit card debt. I had to fire the last guy. I need someone by next week to take over managing the place. I sure don't want to do it. I got a trip to Barbados planned without my wife, which makes it all the more imperative that I go.

"The pay isn't bad, $18.00 an hour. It's not hard work. I just need someone I can trust. The last guy was skimming money. Would you want to move south to the beautiful Georgia coast and quit selling boats to the likes of me?"

I interrupted. "Howard, this is Trent. Tell me about the job." Jackson regarded me with a baffled expression.

"Presently, we lease thirty-three slips, which is full capacity. Basically, you are your own boss. The finances are the main thing. You make sure the bills are paid and that the money is collected. You supervise a couple of college kids that do the manual labor."

"What if I lack boat knowledge?"

"Nobody expects you to repair anything. Something breaks down I have a list of people. You call the appropriate one. Now, if I remember correctly, Jackson told me that you are in charge of the Park on the island and that you have been there for a long time."

"That's right."

"Well, I don't want to be nosy, but I would say it is safe to say you make more than $18.00 an hour."

"I would like a change of scenery. Look, we can get off the speakerphone, and you can ask Jackson anything you want about me."

"I don't need to do that. He's mentioned you several times over the years. Says if you told him the Atlantic Ocean had dried up that he would slash boat prices and get out of business without driving across the bridge to look. I don't want to see you do something that you will regret later. Why don't you think about it?"

"Do I have your word that you won't hire someone else until you hear from me?"

"You certainly do. But I need to know within two days."

"That's okay. I understand. What about benefits?"

"How about three weeks off a year and health insurance, but don't expect the policy to match the one you have with the town."

The frown on Jackson's face had not departed since I interrupted their conversation. "Howard, I'll call you in a couple of days and let you know when I will deliver the boat."

"That sounds like a deal. See you later, Jackson. Hope to hear from you, Trent, but think it through." He paused for several moments before adding, "This is about a woman, isn't it?"

"Partly."

"Son, never allow a woman inside of your heart." The phone clicked off.

"Don't do this," Jackson said tersely. "Things will pick up. It's just a bad time."

"Jackson, try to understand. I want out of here, and this is my chance."

"Your son, family, friends, your way of life is all tied to here. Don't do this over Alex."

"It's more than that. Look, I can't explain it, but please try to understand. I feel like I'm going to die if I stay here. Every day I think about checking out."

He sat down on that one.

I reached into my pocket and showed him a small brown plastic bottle. I shook them for effect. "Anti-depressant pills. I've always fought through the darkness when it hit but I allowed my well-intended doctor to talk me into taking this crap. Minimal side effects, right."

"What does it do to you?" he asked, his voice low, as he rubbed his hands together slowly.

"I don't feel anymore. I stand over the toilet and wait five minutes to pee. I become dizzy if I move quickly and when I try to read, it's like the words are shaking back and forth. Best of all, it wires me like a dozen hits of speed. I know that half of the United States is on this type of drug but look at this." I hold my arm out. My hand shakes as I fight to control it. "Help me get out of here. Even if you don't understand. Even if you think that it's wrong. Please help me. I'm going to do what I can to take the job anyway, with or without your help."

He stared at me for several moments. Slowly he nodded. "I'll do what I can."

"You always have."

The next day I drove to Anne's house. She was the mother of my son and my ex-wife. I informed them that I was moving to Georgia. I gave her a check for $25,000 along with a piece of paper drafted that morning by my attorney stating that this was child support for the next four years when Brooks will be eighteen and our legal agreements ended.

Brooks looked at her and said firmly, "Do it, Mom."

She signed it and returned the paper.

Brooks hugged me and told me that he understood. Knowing that I planned to change my phone number, I tell him if he needs me to call Jackson.

My condo had been on the market since I moved in with Alex. I called my realtor and told her to lower the price by $10,000, and she quickly found a buyer. I was taking a loss, but at least I was free from the mortgage debt. I purchased a used Nissan Z.I was left with $5,000, my partial pension, and 401k funds.

It was early the next week when I left Mom standing in the driveway crying. Most of my meager possessions had been stored in their garage since Alex and I split. I asked her to sell everything and put the money in a savings account that I opened for Brooks when he was little. Nobody outside of Jackson knew of my exact destination. It was how I wanted it.

I stopped by his office before parting. He saw me through the office window and walked outside. "Packed and ready?"

I nodded. "I'll see you next week when you bring the boat down."

He nodded his head slowly. "I don't know what to say."

"I know."

"I wish I could say I understand but I don't. I just hope that you know what you are doing."

"It has to be better than remaining here."

"Okay, one more thing. I talked to Howard late last night. The pay is now $20.00 per hour, and he owns a condo that you can stay in. You just pay utilities and minimal rent."

"That sounds good. I need to get on the road." We embraced and held each other tightly.

He turned and walked toward his office. "It won't be the same around here."

I drove across the drawbridge and entered Wrightsville Beach. I circled the loop one last time. As I approached the drawbridge to leave, I fumbled inside my backpack that rested on the passenger seat. I pulled the bottle of anti-depressant pills from it and at the peak of the bridge; I tossed them with my left hand over my car and the silver guard railing. Before they hit the water, I felt the first sliver of hope that I have felt in over a month.

9

Scattered etches of brilliant orange highlighted the mostly dark sky as I ran the loop in an attempt to sweat the tequila from my body. My thoughts drifted to the previous night, chiefly concerning Jackson. He was in rare form. I can't get accustomed to the depth of matters he wants to discuss. Conversations that he once rolled his eyes at me for introducing, he institutes. Last night he placed his hand on my shoulder after a vain attempt to catch up with me in tequila consumption and said, "I've seen you love two women. Two women that you had to convince to abandon their own comfortable life to let go and fall in love with you. Next time, find a woman that already lives from her heart the way that you do."

My run was complete. I walked the steps to the deck-I observed the hue of pink light hovering over the marshes. The sun was about to emerge. Jackson sat on the deck as I approached. He stood and said, "I'll cook some breakfast." He paused before adding, "Unless you want to start in with shots of tequila again."

"Breakfast will do for a start." I turned and looked out at the water, hearing the door close behind me. "What tequila shots?" I whispered.

It was past ten when I departed. I felt better now that I had purged some of the iniquity from my body. I ate lightly with Jackson before he left for work. As I approached the drawbridge, it dawned on me that I'm actually hungry. I know just where to stop.

There is a strip mall just on the other side of the bridge, with a bagel place that I once frequented every morning on my way to work.

I entered the store as if I just absconded yesterday. It is best that I am confident before the owner, Ivan, saw me. He was behind the counter, taking an order from three girls, all blondes and probably students at the local university.

Behind Ivan and to his right was Jimmy, his assistant. Jimmy looked barely old enough for high school, but he was married with a four-year-old son. He stood a good six feet tall and was so gangly that he reminded me of an undeveloped freshman high school basketball player.

Ivan still had not spotted me as I fell in line to the left of the girls. "Jimmy," I called out. "I'll take the usual."

He turned and his face transformed from annoyance to surprise.

Ivan looked up. His scrutiny shifted to annoyance. He also looked up because he was so short that the three college girls towered over him. He was a stout man with slightly thinning hair the color of coal, a prominent nose, a strong square chin, and an always present three-day beard. He was still about forty pounds too heavy.

I knew he would speak to me through the girls in front of him. It was his way. The poor girls don't know it yet, but they would be the instrument he would play simply because they are in harm's way. I braced for his heavy Russian accent that I once struggled mightily to understand. That is okay. He probably labored to understand my southern drawl.

He paused for effect. "What do you ladies think of someone who comes to your store every day and then one day just disappears? Poof, he is gone." He raised his arms, flapping them slightly as if he was flying away. "I asked around to see if anyone knows what became of the man who runs the Park on the island. I scanned the obituaries each day. Rumors are rampant. I heard that he left town over a woman, but I say to my wife, how could this be so? A tall, handsome man like him would not let one beautiful woman take him down. He could have more. So many more," he said lowering his voice and shaking his head in dismay as he gazed toward the ceiling as if it might hold the answers.

The girls turned and looked at me. I'm too old to be considered good-looking to a college girl. My ego accepted this.

He gave them their order in one large paper bag. He shook his head in disgust. "When I heard that he and his lady friend split, I offered to fix him up with a friend of mine. Very pretty girl. Everyone says so. He is too afraid to meet her. Part man, part chicken. Don't you ladies agree?"

The girls paid for their order and hastily escaped. One of them looked at me with compassion and paused to touch my arm. I don't know if it was because of my looks he had so generously overrated or sympathy that I will be left alone to endure the brunt of his assault. It was probably the latter.

I don't know why he ever took such an interest in me. He often bitched at me for feeling sorry about myself. He was one of those people that never allowed a bad break to knock them down. He would always be fighting and clawing his way back. I admired that in him greatly. I have found the power to fight back, but often it took time to find my second wind. He was born with a second, and a third, a fourth.

"Could I get the usual?"

He shook his head and turned to Jimmy. "Guy comes here for the first time in two years, and he wants the usual. Like I remember what the usual is."

"Egg—"

He turned quickly. His eyes filled with feigned fury. "Don't push it, or you will pay double today." We are both *Seinfeld* fans. His favorite episode was "The Soup Nazi," and he often liked to play the role as he was now.

He started to write on his pad. "Egg, pepper jack cheese, and a mushroom on a spinach bagel toasted." It was never mushrooms. It was always "a mushroom," enriched with his ponderous accent.

Jimmy already had it prepared. He placed it on the counter.

Ivan's dark eyes narrowed. "Don't even try to ask for it to go, my former friend."

"You think I could maybe get something to drink with it?"

He turned to Jimmy and shook his head. "And now he wants something to drink. What next?"

He walked around to the cooler and retrieved a Snapple, Orangeade. He placed it on the counter. I held a twenty-dollar bill out for him to take.

He turned to Jimmy once again; he began to speak in an unknown tongue. Jimmy looked at me with amusement. That was with good reason. Ivan had unknowingly returned to his native dialogue.

He was at the end of the counter now. He turned, looking at me and then to Jimmy. Finally, he spoke in English. "And now he insults me by trying to pay." He pointed his stout hand at me. "You pay me next time, my friend. Now let us sit. We shall talk." It might be an hour before I get out of here. But it will be time well spent.

I told him where I was living and why I was back. He listened with concern but most of all; he wanted to know why I left.

"Alex came in here after you left. Beautiful girl," he said with a heavy sigh. "She made a big mistake, you know?"

When I failed to respond, he touched my arm. "I think that she did, my friend. You should think so as well."

I shook my head, daring to disagree with him.

He shook his head tightly. "Don't put yourself down, my friend." He rose to wait on a line of customers.

***

It was eleven when I arrived at my parent's home. Mom was busy putting items into a small faded gold-colored suitcase that was probably forty years old. Dad was motionless in the recliner. He was pale, and I couldn't detect any sign of breathing.

"Dad," I called softly.

There was no response. "Dad," I said again louder.

He opened his right eye slowly, leaving the left one closed. He was barely audible as he spoke, but there was an unmistakable brief spark in his eyes. "I'm just laying here worrying about my $400.00."

I would have laughed so hard that I might have busted a rib if I had not just thought that I had discovered a dead man in the recliner.

I sat on the couch. "That was pretty good, Dad."

He smiled slightly. "I'm ready to go to the hospital. I think that I would have been better by now if they would have left me there."

I nodded, not to agree, but just to acknowledge that I heard him. He wanted to believe that they might fix him one more time.

His next words were closer to the truth of how he really felt. "All of my tools are in the garage." Moments passed before he snapped his fingers together slightly. "My tool pouch is behind the seat of my truck."

"Going somewhere?" I asked. I guess that with four daughters and one son, I was a shoo-in for the tools.

His fingers interlocked together, and he twiddled his thumbs in a circular motion around each other. It was yet another one of the habits of a man who had changed so little in his lifetime.

"You should come back home," he stated.

"I'm here now."

"I mean for good."

He pointed his index finger at me like a little kid playing with a toy gun. It doesn't offend me the way it usually did. I cut him off. "Dad, I'm forty-three. When have I ever listened to you?" I chuckled and to my surprise, he laughed slowly and said no more.

At five minutes past twelve, two EMTs, one female with bleached blonde hair and wide hips, and one balding, skinny male, gingerly placed him in the back of the ambulance. Mom stood with me in the driveway. The male EMT called my name and waved for me to come over. I walked to him. "Your dad wants to speak with you."

I hopped up into the back of the ambulance. He was lying on the stretcher, clad in old soft blue pajamas. "Drive your mama to the hospital. She doesn't need to drive."

Always his concern is for her. He had loved her and protected her for almost six decades. He was not prepared to relinquish his job just yet.

I nodded gently. "I will." I stepped back outside. The doors closed. Mom and I watched the ambulance depart.

10

I dreamed that as far as the eye could see, candles glowed softly. Alex emerged from the center of my vision. She wore one of her signature long flowing dresses. She walked toward me. She did not stride with daintiness but rather with purpose as if she was trying to outpace her beauty, her sexiness. She failed every time. She smiled and beckoned for me to join her. And then she brusquely vanished. I woke with a start.

It was five a.m. What a way to begin the day. I rose and walked outside onto the deck. The clear dark sky was lit up with stars. The moon not quite full. Across the narrow body of water, a lady, gently illuminated by elegantly done landscape lighting sat in a white rocking chair on her deck. She wore a royal blue bathrobe. Her dark hair was shoulder length. She gently sipped from a bright yellow coffee mug. She smiled slightly in my direction. Her attention returned to something in her hand. Soft light flashed for a moment, and I realized that she was reading from some sort of tablet. I speculated as to whether this is her routine or was she also stirred by a dream of bygone moments of another time and place?

I know where the dream of endless candles derived from, and though I don't want to revisit that time, my memory took me there without my permission.

I walked down the center aisle toward her. Alex smiled so happily. We were in a large metal warehouse located in a small town in the mountains of North Carolina. The floor was bare concrete. Every type of candle imaginable surrounded us. Initially, she picked up one small basket. Now we had two grocery carts that were almost full. She continued to smile as I approached her.

She was conservative with her shopping until she entered the roped-off section. A female employee handed her a huge paper sack and said, "Fill it up, sweetie. Twenty dollars a bag."

I stopped short of her. The aroma of thousands of candles under one roof slightly disturbed my sinuses. Still, I would allow nothing to damper this moment.

"Tell the truth. You want me so badly right now that you can't stand it," she said as she placed her hand on my chest.

"I might ask the lady if they have a back room."

She hugged me tightly. "Thank you. No one has ever brought me to a candle factory before."

We stayed in a house in Blowing Rock that rested on the edge of a mountain. The view spectacular. Each night we sat in the small glassed-in room adjacent to the kitchen. We ate dinner, drank red wine and talked. Last night she shocked me by saying that she did not know when, but she was confident that we would be married. Finally, after all the broken roads of my life, could I be settling down with this beautiful woman, who seemed to have changed her world to coincide with mine?

I heard the glass door slide behind me, interrupting my reminiscing of times long ago vanished. Jackson placed two mugs of coffee on the rail. "Thought you could use a cup."

I sipped from the brown mug and was surprised that it tasted good. Maybe I could graduate from Diet Sun Drops in the morning to coffee. It seemed so adult.

"Why are you up so early?"

He sipped from his coffee mug and said, "I was thirsty, and I went to the kitchen for a drink of water. I saw you standing out here. I had to be up early anyway. I have to check on a boat in Morehead City."

"I had a nightmare," I said.

The lady in the royal blue robe rose from her chair and disappeared inside. We stood in silence sipping our coffee. Jackson took my mug and walked toward the door. "I'll have another one," I said.

He returned and we sat in the stillness of the morning until the first pink hues of false dawn appeared over the marshes. Birds serenaded us. Lights came on in three of the houses across the canal.

Elton John was singing faintly, "Don't Let the Sun Go Down on me." I walked inside and retrieved my phone, checked the display, and clicked the call off. I placed it on the railing beside my coffee mug.

Elton sang again, five minutes later. I answered.

"When are you coming home?"

"Not for a while. Problems?"

"No problems. I just miss you."

There was quietness as I struggled for a response.

"I was looking forward to having some fun while my schedule was free."

"I kind of have some things going on here," I answered tersely.

"How is your father?" she asked as an afterthought.

I choose not to respond, knowing that she could care less. Aware that she was concerned about little except the games she played to get herself through each day.

"Don't you think you should have seen me before leaving so abruptly? I'm your boss."

"My boss is in Greece," I countered.

"Yes, with the blonde. I know all about it. How long will you be there?"

"I don't know. I'll call you when I know more."

"Don't hang up."

"Bye," I stated firmly, ending the call.

I stood and drank my coffee and returned the mug to the rail. The homes across the canal began to come to life with light as people started their day. In one yard, an annoying gray poodle barked at a large tabby cat. The cat looked as if it was prepared to smack the intruder into the water if it drew one pace nearer, and even though I'm no fan of felines, I found myself pulling for the cat.

"Something about work?" Jackson asked.

I never lie to Jackson. Hesitating, I debated as to whether or not saying yes was a lie.

"It was Howard's wife, Brenda," he said, more statement than question.

I nodded slightly.

"I often wondered what their deal is. They've been married for thirty years and according to Howard, they have been unhappy for a long time. He runs around with younger women, and she has to know. It's not as if he is very discreet about it." He placed his cup back on the railing in front of us. "She may be in her early fifties, but she's still a knockout. Playing tennis sure hasn't hurt her legs. And that long curly hair."

Brenda's long light brown hair was streaked with blond highlights. Age had done little to diminish her body. Her face bore only faint traces of age in the corner of her eyes.

"I always thought that while she's not beautiful that there was a sexiness about her that can't be explained, but it is always present," Jackson added.

I nodded as I reached for my coffee and desired the conversation to end.

"So, how long have you been sleeping with her?"

Stunned, I dropped the ceramic mug. It crashed loudly on the brick patio below us. I shook my head in disbelief. I speculated as to what he was thinking. Howard was a friend of his. Not friends like we are but still a friend. A friend that he convinced to give me a job. I struggled for words, but I came up empty.

"You can stop beating yourself up," he said.

"But he is your friend, Jackson."

"He's been cheating on her for decades. What am I going to do, condemn her?"

"No. Me."

"It's not the brightest thing that you have ever done, but this ain't church, and I ain't the preacher."

"How long have you known?"

"Remember when I came to see you the last time? You being the hugger you are, I caught the briefest hint of Clinique in the air. She wears it."

I looked at him incredulously. "You are a perfume expert now?"

"I stopped by to see Howard on my way to your place. She walked in and hugged me." It's so much like Jackson to hold information for months and feel no need to share. It's yet another reason that I trust him more than anyone in this world.

"In answer to your earlier question, I think that perhaps they stay together to keep from dividing assets. I see a lot of that in my line of work. More of a business arrangement than a marriage." He paused. "Talk to me. I know this bothers you."

"It does."

"When did it start?"

I sighed deeply and began to tell him of the night I ventured down yet another wrong path in a lifespan of injudicious steps.

***

There was a tap on the office glass door. Brenda stood there wearing a black tennis outfit. Her muscular legs glistened with a mixture of sweat and water from the rain that began falling an hour ago. I opened the door.

"Working late, aren't you?"

"The computer has been down much of the day. Just trying to catch up."

She walked to the small kitchen, opened the fridge, and retrieved a beer. She opened it and drank heartily.

"I had a few glasses of wine with the girls after our tennis match." She paused before asking, "Are you almost through?"

I rubbed my eyes. "Yes."

She smiled and said, "I left the club and saw your car. Driving ten blocks was difficult enough. Ten miles, well, would you be a dear and drive me home? I would call Howard, but he's out of town."

"Sure. Give me about ten minutes."

She sat on the couch across from me. "You are a strange one, Trent Mullins. You don't drink. You don't socialize. You work, exercise at that fitness club on Third Street, and live at that shack in the middle of nowhere all by yourself."

I stopped typing, feeling my eyes squint as I looked at her, and then I looked down and began typing again. Minutes later, I stopped.

"Let's go," I said as I rose.

She held her hand out for me to help her up. I pulled gently, and when she stood, she fell into my chest. She pulled away and looked up at me with an impish grin.

We walked outside to my car. The rain had just stopped but it appeared as if more might be on the way.

"Please put the top down. I want to feel the fresh air."

I opened her door, walked around, got in, and started the engine. I pushed the button to put the top down.

"Been a long time since a man opened a car door for me." She allowed her tennis skirt to ride so high that I could see the black tights underneath. "Am I still an attractive woman, Trent?"

The look on her face flashed quickly from mischief to a glimpse of apprehension. It was as if she had blinked and woken much older than she ever dreamed she would be.

"Yes."

She smiled appreciatively.

Stone walls bordered the winding driveway to their home. Small dome-shaped lights sat atop of them. Both seemed out of place. Palm trees lined both sides of the drive. The landscape looked gaudy and pretentious. Maybe that is what rich people do to camouflage the discontent of their voyage.

"Come inside," she said. She saw the hesitation on my face. "It's not polite to fail to see a girl home safely." I followed her, knowing that it was a bad idea.

The gigantic house was decorated extravagantly. Oil paintings on every wall. The dining room alone was near the size of the shack. She walked into the kitchen. "I'm going to brew some cappuccino. Have one with me?" She didn't wait for an answer.

She returned and said, "It will be ready in a few minutes. I'm going to shower." She smiled as her eyes glinted with playfulness. "Don't go anywhere." She climbed the stairs, looking back once to ensure that I had not moved.

I knew I should leave. Being the fool that I am. I remained frozen in place.

Minutes later she returned. She was clad in a black cotton robe. Her long hair was dripping wet. She shook it to each side, wringing out some of the excess water, as she walked into the kitchen. I heard the spoon clatter against the cups. I sat awkwardly at one end of the colossal teal couch.

She gave me the cup of cappuccino and placed her cup on the walnut table in front of us as she sat in the middle of the couch. We drank the cappuccino and chatted about tennis, the marina, and Jackson.

She rose and walked to the large window that took up half of the room. "On a clear night, you can see the white from the waves." She turned back to me and smiled. I watched as she loosened the sash around her robe. She opened it and dropped it to the floor.

I struggled for something to say. It had been almost a year since I had been with Alex. There had been no one else. I placed the cup on the table as I rose from the couch. "I'm leaving, Brenda."

"You don't want to do that."

"You are married and drunk."

Jackson looked at me without interrupting. He knew there was more to the story and he waited patiently for it.

It was early the next morning before the sun was up. I thought that I heard the door open and I wondered if I had locked the door. The lock didn't half work anyway. I fell back asleep.

I woke minutes later. I could smell her perfume and then she was in my bed. I wanted to tell her to stop, but it had been too long.

Minutes later, she kissed me and said assuredly, "I always get my way."

I turned back to Jackson. "That is how it started and once it did, I didn't know how to stop it."

"Did you want to end it?"

"Yes," I answered too eagerly before adding, "and no."

"Do you think that she makes a regular practice of it?"

"I don't know. She says not."

"You sure can land in some precarious positions."

"That I can," I said, my lips pursed.

"She broke you down."

I breathed in deeply and then exhaled. "There is one good thing. It's all physical, and that keeps things from being complicated."

"Yeah," he agreed with a nod. "Too bad it's not what you have wanted since the day I met you."

I started to respond but we're interrupted by the sound of footsteps at the bottom of the stairs. The methodical march continued, and when they ended, there was the anguished face of a son that I had not seen since my hasty departure.

11

The boy in front of me was on the threshold of becoming a young man. He was taller than I expected, just shy of six feet. One thing that had not changed was the soft brown eyes that highlighted his smooth, handsome face. Eyes blended with pain and anger. They held water that he fought desperately to cling to. Neither of us moved. Neither of us sure what we were supposed to do at this moment.

Jackson walked toward him. He had been in Brooks' life since he was three years old. I watched as Jackson's right hand lightly gripped the side of my son's head. Brooks' eyes grew more prominent as he looked at Jackson, and then they narrowed as they returned to me. Jackson walked inside, leaving us alone.

The injury in his eyes transported me to another time when my decisions inflicted great anguish on him. It was a pain that will haunt me until my last breath.

***

It was early Sunday morning, my son's birthday weekend. I have penitence for screwing up special occasions. He sat in the room that Alex had told him months earlier was his. But that was coming to an end. This would be our last day together.

She touched my arm as she passed by me. We loved each other, but she had invented many reasons why that was not enough. I know there was nothing that I can say that would change her mind, and I did not wish to try.

Brooks was seated at the computer playing on the Internet. She wrapped her arms tightly around him. He held her arms with his hands. Both of them wept.

It was more than I could bear. I walked through the living area to the bedroom and entered the large bathroom. I sat on the cold gray tile floor. I wrapped my arms around my knees. Tears flowed from a seemingly endless reservoir.

She stated this morning that she had no regrets about anything in her life. I said that I don't believe anyone who said that. It was just one of those things that we attempt to sell ourselves, believing that saying it often enough will make it true. I knew there was injury in my son's eyes. I was filled with remorse and guilt because he was my responsibility. I can't let myself off the hook with a convenient no regret policy.

It was not the moment described that will torture me the most on this forlorn day or stay forever engraved in my mind. It was later when we prepared to leave her house for the last time. She had taken him shopping for his birthday present as I packed away some of our things. When they returned he showed me the new watch that she had bought him, but the angry red welts under his eyes was what I would never be free from.

The three of us walked toward the front door. She told him that they would soon see each other, but it was just an attempt to make a deplorable situation somewhat better.

I know that it took a lot for her to open her home and heart to not only me but to my son. She had never dated anyone with a child before. I know that she loved Brooks more than she ever dreamed she would.

He loved her far more than any other woman that I dated. She hugged him tightly but released him abruptly. Her quota of tears had been reached for the day; everything in her life analytical.

She kissed me goodbye and turned away as if I was already a distant memory. We stepped away. The door closed softly but firmly behind us.

***

He bit his lower lip, his body visibly trembled.

"I know that there is nothing I can say to make any of this right."

"No shit, Dad," he replied as he inserted his hands into his pockets. "I never thought that you were leaving for good."

He wanted answers. Answers that I knew would not be good enough for him or me.

"Why, Dad? Why just drop out of my life completely?"

I breathed deeply. "Every day, I would think that it was the day to call you, but I thought I had done too much damage. I never planned it this way."

"It wasn't your fault that you and Alex split. It was her fault."

"No. She had good reasons. She was right. I'm not driven for success the way she is. I don't care about moving to bigger cities for better opportunities. I don't yearn to travel the world."

"That doesn't mean anything."

"You're right. It doesn't matter. What does matter is that I hurt you by moving into a woman's house not once but twice. Twice, I got your hopes up, and twice your spirits were crushed. I could never give you what I desired."

I paused and rubbed my hands together, searching for any words that might make sense. "I was in Mom's garage one night right after Alex and I split, boxing all of our stuff away. I packed all of your keepsakes into one box. I sealed it, and then I looked at it, and I said to myself, this is all my son has to show for thirteen years. Everything in one box, and you deserved so much more. It broke me."

"Stuff in a box doesn't matter. A dad that loved and cared about me. You took that."

"You always had a Dad who loved you. I just wasn't here for you. I thought that you were better off without me."

"Let me get this straight. You left to protect me? Thanks for nothing."

His cheeks flushed with fury. Tears finally made their escape. "I got news for you, Dad. The hurt you caused by leaving was a million times worse than a box of stuff."

He was halfway down the steps before I breathed again. He came here to inflict injury, and he proved successful. He was also accurate in everything he stated. I heard a car start up and leave. I wondered how he got here. Not his mom, I reasoned. Probably his best friend, Anna.

I was vaguely aware of the sliding door opening and then closing as I stared blankly out at the water. Jackson's strong hands gripped my shoulders. "This can be fixed. He loves you as much as ever, maybe more."

I had no words to offer to the conversation.

He patted my upper chest several times with each hand before leaving me to drown in the blackness of my ruminations.

***

It was mid-afternoon when I drove toward the hospital.

Lately, I've been running on faith. What else can a poor boy do?

I smiled at the words Eric Clapton offered. My thoughts drifted back to my father and then quickly to my son. What would my son think when my time to depart this earth came? Would amends have been made? As far as my father was concerned, one of my biggest fears was that I would feel nothing when his time came.

It always amazed me that I could feel so deeply about so much, and he seemingly felt little of anything except a need to be the center of attention. But he loved my mom, as I do, and he made her life as easy as possible. He could have done no more for her than he did. I prefer to think of that right now and not on the fact that we really never had one single dialogue of any depth.

12

The rain that moved into the area in mid-afternoon had lowered the temperature over ten degrees since Moses and Maybelle had walked home from church. Moses sat on the front porch and listened to the rain fall through the two gigantic live oaks that dominated the landscape in front of him. His grandfather had planted those trees over a century ago.

His father built the two-story, two thousand-plus-square foot-home almost seventy-five years ago. Like most homes of that age, there had been several renovations along the way, most of which Moses accomplished with the help of family and friends. That was how it was in Dylan Town. Neighbors still relied on each other, though Moses recognized that time was slowly decaying their little community as the children grew up and left for the dazzling lights and opportunities that the bigger cities like Atlanta offered.

Moses and Maybelle moved into this house almost thirty years ago, not long after his dad passed away. His mom didn't want to live alone in this big old house as she called it. She moved to Norcross to live with her sister, who was also a widow.

The first home that Moses and Maybelle lived in was barely one-thousand-square feet. It was okay in the early years when it was just the two of them but when two children arrived into this world, it made for tight quarters.

The first renovation they tackled before moving in was the biggest. They flipped the house, not like today, with people trying to make quick money by fixing a place and then selling it. Maybelle insisted that the front porch be where Moses could not view the store, which was about a quarter of a mile away. She had watched his daddy try to relax while sitting on the porch but with the store in his vision, it led him to contemplate about all the work he needed to do.

Moses smiled as he recalled her saying, "Moses Dylan, you are a hard-working man, and you do well by our children and me but when you are home, I want you home with us. Not peering down the drive and thinking about what needs to be done at that store."

The bedrooms were all upstairs, and the bottom floor had been a kitchen, dining, living, and half bath. Maybelle also wanted their home to be more open. She didn't want to be cooking in a small kitchen while the family was in another room. They opened it up into one big kitchen, dining, and living area, which contained the restored fireplace. The half bath remained. She told Moses, "That way, I can look at your fine self when I am fixing dinner." She also wouldn't allow but a stoop to the now back door entrance. "We will be a front porch sitting family," she stated with no room for deliberation.

He heard her soft steps on the wooden floor and then they stopped. Her arms were around his neck, and she hugged him gently. He patted her arm several times. "Sit with me," he said as he gestured toward the empty chair beside him.

They sat together like that for several minutes. She placed her hand on top of his, and he looked admirably at her and smiled. "You still want me to grill chicken?"

"We can have it tomorrow. I pulled one of the chili containers out of the freezer. This cool weather and all, I thought it might prove to be good chili eating weather at least once more before the summer heat sets in."

He nodded his head. "That sounds good."

He heard a chicken squawk and looked through the trees at the weathered gray barn that held equipment, tools, and their egg-laying hens.

He pointed in the direction of the trees that shielded a parcel of land that once held such hope, such promise. "One of your cousins asked me not long ago about that two-acre lot that we hoped that..." He did not finish the statement because of the injury in her eyes. They were given two sons, and they lost one. The child that would return and run the store with his father when his military career was complete. But he would never return and build a home for his family on the lot that was staked out and surveyed years ago.

"We could use the money, but we don't have to sell it."

He nodded and rubbed his chin. "It won't be to your cousin, Alvin. He wanted us to finance the land for him, and not only that, he asked if I could cosign a loan for him to build the house as well. Who am I? Bill Gates?"

"Oh, Alvin," she said with a dismissive shake of her head. "That boy never met a job he wouldn't walk away from."

There was silence again as they sat with their hands intertwined. She cleared her throat. He knew she had something weighing on her mind that needed saying. He could wait. Another minute passed as the rain intensified.

"I will abide by your wishes, Moses."

"What wishes are they?"

"You can evict Trent when he returns."

He looked at her, and she nodded tightly and then returned to watching the rain. There was a sadness impressed upon her face and the resignation that somehow, she had failed.

"You can't save them all, Maybelle."

She barely nodded.

He did indeed want Trent gone, but he sure didn't like the look on his sweet wife's face. He grasped her hand. "You are the finest woman I have ever known, and I'm a blessed man to have your love."

She turned her head slightly and smiled her gratitude. She chuckled and then said, "I guess if he wanted to hold our feet to the fire, legally, we can't evict a man for having a woman spend the night. Even if she is married."

They heard the hum of a small plane off in the distance. "Maybe I should have backed away from trying to save him as you say. I can't save anyone. We both know that only God can accomplish that. I just wanted to lend him some encouragement."

"You always have to try. That's who you are. It's one of the thousands of things I love about you."

"Maybe it should have been you who did the reaching."

He started to interrupt, but she quieted him with her expression. "I don't mean that as any criticism." She breathed deeply as she searched for the right words. "Moses, he comes in our store six days a week. He needs something from you, or at least I think he does. Maybe he doesn't even realize it."

"I don't know what you mean."

"I see the way he looks at you. He respects you greatly for probably being the man he thinks he can't be. I believe he seeks your approval."

"Well, he's not going to achieve that by sleeping with married women."

"I know he has done wrong. And as I said, you can tell him to leave when he returns. But Moses, if down the road, he ever reaches out to you. Don't be so hard on him. I think he has endured enough of that, and he doesn't need it because no one is harder on him than he is." She paused as Moses considered her words. "I think Trent knows that God will forgive anything but even with that knowledge, there are people in this world that just can't grant that kind of grace to their life."

She stood and moved in front of him. She grasped both his powerful hands in hers and thought of how much she adored this formidable man. He was a man many feared, but he had never proven anything but gentle and protective of her.

"Moses, let's go inside. I want you to hold me."

He nodded, and as he rose, she pretended to be helping him up. He smiled at her feigned effort.

She looked up at him as he stood. "I'm going upstairs to the bedroom and I will wait for you. I want to open the windows and lay with you and listen to the rain falling."

He watched her walk into the house like he had done a million times. She had on a white dress with streaks of teal through it. He smiled and looked to the heavens. "Thank you, Lord."

Later, she laid her head on his mountain of a chest. The rain could be heard through the windows and was accentuated by the metal roof they had installed after the last hurricane removed half the shingles from their roof.

Softly, she said, "I am still going to pray for Trent." She felt his arm pull her in closer. The rhythmic sound of the rain came through the windows and drummed lightly on the roof. His chest rose and fell like waves touching the shore before returning to sea once again. She fell asleep quickly.

***

I walked up the six levels of expansive dull brick steps toward the hospital entrance. A huge fountain dispersed water toward the sky. Each side of the walkway was covered with mature Azalea plants, most in the down cycle of their annual bloom.

I entered the building and walked to the elevators and punched the button for the fifth floor. I walked toward the lobby station and turned right, alone in my thoughts.

"He's making plans," a smiling man said to me as if he had just seen me yesterday. Hayden was in his late sixties and looked every bit of it. He was a medium-framed man with a protruding belly. His hair was thin, a mixture of white and gray. There were dark circles under his eyes that reminded me of a raccoon.

He was one of the few people that could get the best of Dad in a war of words. I had often seen him frustrate Dad so badly that Dad would sit quietly in the corner of Hayden's dispatcher's office. Silencing my old man, as any long-term Wilmington resident could tell you, was no small feat.

Hayden once worked on the island as a dispatcher, back in a time before automated 911 centers took over. Dad and Hayden met many years ago when they both worked in the Fire Department for the city of Wilmington. Dad was nearing the end of his career, and Hayden was in the early stages of his.

Many people found Hayden gruff, and that was their problem and their loss. He just liked to have fun in life and if ruffling your feathers increased the joy of his day, then so be it. Beyond the wisecracks and the harmless insults lay a genuine heart of gold.

He was the epitome of the good neighbor of times long gone when we spent time getting to know our neighbors instead of burying our heads in the latest iPhone. Even better, his neighborhood stretched well beyond his home. As most firemen did in their careers, he had a job on the side. He did household repairs. Painting was the job he was hired for most often, but he was capable with almost any tool.

He once infuriated the chief in the police department with one of his good deeds. He took a job for the chief's elderly mother to paint her small garage. He noticed that her front porch had several soft spots from aged, rotted wood. He questioned her about it, and she told him that her son had been telling her for months that he would do it.

Hayden stopped by her home two weeks later. The porch remained in dire need of repair. He drove to the lumber store and one hour later, he was rebuilding her porch. He finished the job the following day and never took a dime for it.

Upon discovering Hayden's good deed, the chief was incensed and asked him why he had done it. I'm sure there was a grin on Hayden's face when he replied, "Because she would have fallen and broken her hip by the time you peeled yourself away from the golf course to do it."

I extended my hand. "How are you, Hayden?"

He smiled broadly, proudly showing off the slight gap between his front teeth. He took my hand firmly and popped me on top of my shoulder with his other. "Yes sir, he is making plans."

"In control to the very end." I am immediately sorry that I said it. Hayden's eyes lose their sparkle for an instant, but he quickly returned to smiling.

"So, what's the plan?"

"I'm supposed to sell the truck and his handguns. You are to stay here and move in with your mother. He was reading the classifieds. There was a job in the Parks & Recreation Department in the city. Yes sir, he's making plans." Having released my hand, he whacked me on my other shoulder. "Drop by the office tomorrow. I'm cooking chicken and rice," he said as he absentmindedly rubbed his stomach. During his years as a dispatcher, he often cooked lunch for the police department. However, word would leak out and employees from the fire department and town hall would come as well. He would call me to offer an invitation.

"I might just do that."

"You better. I'll see you." He took a step and stopped and turned back. His smile was replaced by a look of gravity. His booming voice barely a whisper. "If you or your mother needs anything, you call me." I nodded and watched him walk away. He disappeared into the elevator.

I continued the journey to Dad's room. Much to my relief, I found him alone. He's sleeping soundly, no doubt exhausted from entertaining Hayden. A large white woman with two chins, watermelon size breasts, and hips ample enough to support the package came in and checked his IV. She departed, never acknowledging my existence.

Dad's eyes flickered, and he smacked his lips together deliberately.

"Water?"

He nodded gently.

I walked to the other side of the bed and retrieved the cup from his table. I scooped ice from the white plastic container into the cup. I poured water from the orange container and stuck the straw in the cup, carefully bending it toward him. I held the cup to his mouth, and he drank slowly. He held his hand up to signal he had enough.

"I saw Hayden."

He nodded. I was confident that he would not share his plans with me. As critical as I am of my father, in some ways, I think that he had us all beat. He did not know what depression was. Worry and stress was something for other people to suffer. I doubted until these past few years when his health began to fail that he ever had a bad day. Some just proved better than others.

He drifted back off to sleep, and I sat beside him for almost an hour. I stood over him and watched him laboring for breath. I nodded softly and walked away.

I drove to Jackson's house. I reached in my pocket and located the key he gave me and let myself in. I called and ordered pizza. I placed my phone on the kitchen counter when it struck me that I have not ordered pizza from this particular restaurant since the night Carmen visited me one last time and tried to coax me to take one more flight with her. In a life filled with risks, it was the one gamble I could not take. Hours later, she was dead, and the woman that I had loved more than life itself was gone forever.

She was on her way back to me, encouraged by Jackson when she collided violently with an SUV. I have frequently deliberated what might have transpired if she had completed her journey back to me that night. Maybe I would have looked into the eyes of the person who knew and understood me the most. Perhaps, I would have once again seen the girl that I fell in love with twice. Once in my youth, when it was against my will. The other, many years later. I have deeply loved two women in my life and been loved in return. Alex began backing away once she discovered all that raged inside of me. That never drove Carmen away. Maybe it was easier for her to understand the turmoil inside me because she never could tame the outcast voices that raged inside her spirit.

It was strange that as often as the past haunted me that the night of her death rarely frequented my thoughts. As far as I know, only Jackson knew that she was on her way back to me when she died in his arms that night on a darkened roadside. It was a subject that we never spoke of after he arrived at my house to inform me of her death. There was a hushed understanding between us that this was the way that we both needed it to be.

I stripped my clothes off and moved inside the shower. I turned the water as hot as I could stand it. Twenty minutes later, I turned the water off and grabbed a towel. The mirrors were fogged from the steam.

I walked to the bedroom that I was sleeping in, clad only with a towel wrapped around my waist. I caught my reflection in the mirror. My hair neared my shoulders and was in need of a trim. I wore a mustache for years, but my face was cleanly shaven since the first gray hairs appeared. No longer do I get stopped in the grocery store and told that I look like Tom Selleck.

Elton sang and I walked to the kitchen counter to retrieve my phone. It was a number that began with an area code that I don't recognize. I hit the end call button. I turned back toward the bedroom, slipped slightly, and my towel came unwrapped and landed on the floor at the exact moment I heard a knock on the sliding glass door.

I wrapped the towel back around me as I turned to the door in hopes that it was Jackson. No such luck. A young female, probably college age, stood outside the door, holding a pizza box, trying to suppress laughter.

Like many beach houses, this one was confusing about which door to approach. There was a door on the driveway side, but it led into the garage, which led to very steep steps to an entrance to the kitchen. She had walked up the outside steps on the waterside of the house.

She was cute, petite, and struck me as the animated type. She possessed beautiful big brown eyes that dominated her face. I can hear Paul Newman in the movie, *Message in a Bottle,* saying, "Young lady, if I was about a hundred fifty years younger, you would be in trouble."

I opened the door. She was blushing. "Your pizza, sir," she said as she gave it to me. "It will be $18.75."

Not only have I come to the door, clad only in a towel. I have come with no money. "Excuse me," I said.

I walked back into the bedroom and retrieved twenty-five dollars from the dresser. "Keep it," I said as I gave it to her.

"Have a good evening." She giggled as she walked away. Maybe she thought that if I was a hundred and fifty years younger, I would be in trouble.

I put on a pair of blue jeans and a long-sleeve white tee shirt. I moved to the small bar in the kitchen and sat on a barstool. Lifting the top of the pizza box, I breathed in the aroma. It was smothered with pepperoni and mushrooms. Two pieces curbed my appetite, and I shut the box tightly. I debated whether to put it in the fridge but decided against it, reasoning that Jackson would be home soon.

Sitting on the couch, I fell asleep quickly, and when I woke, the light of the day had concluded. I put on a black L.L. Bean pullover fleece coat and walked outside. The night was cool and clear. Stars lit up the sky. I went to the garage, retrieved a beach chair, and placed it in the trunk of my car.

Minutes later, I parked on the street where Jackson once lived and walked to the beach. I positioned the chair on the beach midway between the streets and looked out over the ocean. This was the area where my ashes are to be scattered when I leave this earth.

It seemed that I had been in a rush my entire life. Always looking back at the time that has gained on me and somehow trying to find a way to make up for all the botched roads that I traveled down.

This was where I spent glorious summers with my son, Jackson, and a wonderful group of friends. The group had dissipated as we have gone on with the living of life that consumes us, leaving behind memories that we will always cling to with ceaseless smiles. It was where I proposed to Carmen. She wept so hard that she could barely whisper, "Yes."

It was also where under a full moon that I spent a fantastic night with Alex. We drank a bottle of wine and watched a full orange moon hover over the ocean. We talked of a life together and how we would always treasure the sacredness of times such as this.

There was so many of those times stored away for recollection. I drew comfort from some and the disenchantment of shattered fantasies from others. All those times proved a commemoration that I had missed out on what I coveted most in this life. Someone to share and build a life together with. I was a horrible husband in a youthful idiotic rushed attempt at marriage. I always wanted another chance to succeed. Love had proven such scarcity for me, and when unearthed, it was in places it was destined to fail. Maybe I knew this as I journeyed down these roads, but my longing for love and intimacy was more potent than any rational thinking that I may have possessed.

A stray, brief cloud blocked part of the moon's light for a moment. I thought of all the times that I felt that I could reason with God in a particular place like the beach.

Mom assured me that he was always near and that I was never alone. My response was what good was it for him to be there if he would do nothing to aid my flight.

Mom prayed often that I would see things differently, and I wished that I had her faith. She believed that he did so much for us, while I focused on what he did not do. The doors that he refused to open. The pain he refused to soothe.

Through each failure and dark time in my life, I would comfort myself with the belief that it was part of a plan. At some point, life would intertwine, and things would balance out. Love and comfort would replace the pain and emptiness that had enveloped my life.

But eventually, I gave up on such a plan that would make sense of this life. During life's shadowy times that appeared unsolicited it seemed you could pray until your internal organs ruptured, but in the end, the pain, heartbreak, and the black hole of hopelessness just had to wear off.

I was in awe of his creation as I peered out over the ocean. "Take care of the family God during this time, especially Mom and my son. Let him live a long, healthy, happy life. And God please never let him suffer from the horrific disease of depression."

I heard footsteps and Jackson placed a chair beside me and handed a glass to me. He put ice cubes in it and poured Crown Royal over them with a splash of Coke Zero. He made one for him and sat the cooler down beside his chair.

"I thought that you might be here. Thanks for the pizza."

"Thanks for this," I said as I tasted the smooth liquor.

"Your day didn't get off to the best of starts. I thought that you could use it."

I nodded once as I looked toward the next wave.

"He was hurting, but he really was just crying out for his dad." He paused and then slowly began speaking again. "The night that you got so down because of all his things packed away in one box. You gave that boy a lot more than things in a box. You've always been too hard on yourself." He touched his glass to mine in a mock toast. "Lighten up."

We sat silently for a few minutes. "I heard you talking when I approached."

"Praying."

"I thought as much. But you are not depressed now?"

"No."

"What was it like? I mean, I know that I have been sad, but I've seen you, and I know it was different than that."

"You mean you don't think that I could just throw a light switch and make it all go away?"

He didn't respond.

"That was what a lot of people think or they don't see anything in your life that was worth hurting over. I once had a family member say to me during my first great battle with depression. 'Your troubles for mine bud.' "

"Damn." He deliberated before continuing, "Why could you not head it off this time before it took hold of you? I know you told me once that the key was to keep moving."

I failed to contain the ferocity in my voice. "Because it came so damn swiftly that I didn't have time to move. It was the night that Brooks and I moved out of Alex's house. I knew that I was better off without her, but the hurt I caused Brooks. Looking back, I was trying to be perfect for her. Living in her house around her infamous mood swings. I drank before she got there to relax. The nights she came home vibrant, charming, and sexy, I continued to drink to celebrate a good night. The nights she came home and walked by me as if I was an intruder, I continued to drink to ease the tension. It all went downhill when I got that viral infection in my sinuses. Blood coming out of my nose every morning. I lost fifteen pounds in two weeks. The ENT doctor said that he had never seen anything like it before and wanted a second opinion. Then the medicine and those horrible side effects. And not one ounce of compassion from her. It was as if it was my fault that I was sick.

"It wasn't like I was lying around whining. I only missed a half-day of work the entire time. I even managed to drag myself to the gym and make it through a workout three times a week.

"One morning, she came back from her morning run. I was on the couch. I had showered and dressed for work and then collapsed. She walked in and looked at me like I was a worthless slug. I drove to my parents' house, slept on their couch for three hours, and went to the doctor.

"Later, she complained that I ran to my mom when I was sick. Can you believe that?"

"I guess the answer to your question was that I was emotionally exhausted by the time the split came and the gas tank was on empty. I had nothing to battle with, and I stupidly allowed my doctor to talk me into trying antidepressants. Minimal side effects. Yeah, right."

I took a sip from my drink and continued. "This whole chemical imbalance thing I've yet to understand." I held my hands up at different levels, the right one higher than the left. "The doctors and more importantly, the pharmaceutical corporations who make millions annually portray their magical little pills like this."

I continued to hold my hands out. "Here was the imbalance; take the pills, and like magic, here was what occurs." I moved both my hands until they were even with each other. "Everything nicely balances out.

"The trouble was how do they know it was a chemical imbalance? In my case, I have had four episodes in my life. The last two were longer and harder, and that is the scary part. That they keep getting worse, and I'm afraid that it may prove to be a continuing pattern.

"And if I have an imbalance, why have I not been clinically depressed every day for most of my life? Why is mine tied to some sequence of emotional events?"

"Tell me what it's like."

I breathed deeply. "Waking early in the morning after fragments of tormented sleep. Afraid to face the day. Each day a marathon. Life moves at the pace of a caterpillar's crawl while my mind races like a runaway Ferris wheel.

The same thoughts repeated a thousand times a day. The fear that my mind may snap like a pretzel."

He fixed another drink for each of us. Jackson amazed me. Here was something that he had not experienced and unlike most people, he refused to criticize what he couldn't understand. He tried to help and what he never failed me with was his total lack of judgment.

"You know that it was not your fault that you got sick, don't you? I mean when you were living with Alex."

"I think that even I understand that," I said dryly.

We became silent once again for several minutes. He drained the remnants of his drink and prepared another for each of us.

"There is a good side to depression."

I could sense the puzzled look on his face as he turned to me in the darkness.

"When I am in a happy time, I treasure it so much because I know the depths of the other side. The trouble is I can't trust happiness. It is fleeting."

His voice was even as he responded moments later. "I understand that. You were so happy when Alex and you were falling in love. I wish I could see you like that more often." He drank again. "What I really wish is that I could see you like that all the time." He gazed out at the ocean as he added. "Care for an observation?"

I raised my glass and motioned for him to proceed.

"Carmen and Alex fell in love with you because of how you made them feel about themselves. I have heard you describe the first time that Carmen and you fell in love. It seems that she fell in love with you because of how she felt about you."

I nodded softly. "Wow."

"What?"

"I thought I was the introspective one."

"You think that I'm right?" he asked as he sat his glass down on the cooler.

"I do."

He fixed another drink for us. "About the depression, I have a cousin that the medication did wonders for."

"While I do think it is terribly overprescribed, I know that it does help certain people, but for me, the side effects just made everything worse. Originally, the doctor sold me on the idea that it would help me sleep but in reality, it was just the opposite."

"Did you ever try to talk to someone about it? I mean besides your regular doctor?"

"Besides you?"

He smiled. "Yes, like a psychologist."

"Not by design," I answered.

13

My childhood was less than ideal and not the Norman Rockwell portrait that my mother so skillfully brushed like an artist in front of a canvas. The picture my mom created for our family existed only within the boundaries of her mind, and I suspect during her moments of halcyon rumination that she recognized this.

Still, I lived my adult life believing that little of my youth was of consequence. Maybe it was the power of positive thinking or my naiveté to assume that I was above possible penalty suffered from a father who reminded you of all that he did for you but could never concede his deficiencies as a verbally abusive parent.

Perhaps it was ingrained in me as a man to think that my strength should render any problem helpless. During my first two battles of depression, I was strong enough to walk out of it when I chose to. After all, I handled every drug imaginable in my youth, and wasn't depression just one more battle of wills fought within the periphery of our mind? But after Carmen and I split I could not walk away clean. I was reduced from the formidable man I viewed myself to be.

Jackson prepared another drink that neither of us needed. His question about seeking help took me to a time when I did reach out to a professional, though it was not a path that I chose of my own accord.

It was the middle of January and my first winter in Georgia. Atlantic Coast Conference Basketball was in full swing. The shack lacking the technology for me to watch games led me to venture out to a bar in Brunswick to watch Duke play Georgia Tech. The bar was dark, drab, and soiled with the odors of alcohol, nicotine, and testosterone. There were seven tables and an L-shaped bar. The owner and operator, Stan, served mixed drinks, beer, and spicy chicken wings that would make your forehead sweat.

Being on the wagon had not exactly endeared me to Stan. Whether I desired them or not, I ordered chicken wings each time I frequented his establishment. That, along with a couple of soft drinks and a generous tip, kept Stan from evicting me.

Actually, he was a pretty nice guy. Heavyset, with three chins, a persistent three-day-old dark beard, and black hair swept back with a heavy gel. Like many people I have encountered, he projected a tough image but underneath seemed to be a decent guy.

The tables were all spoken for when I arrived minutes before tip-off. I moved to the bar and sat beside a man who looked out of place in a tavern usually filled with people who derived their living from the sea. He was nursing a draft beer and a plate of chicken wings.

"You wanna another beer, HD?" Stan asked. The beer is on the bar before the man can respond.

"So, miss tee teetotaler, what will it be?" he asked in a mocking falsetto voice as he stared intently at me. His eyes were dark, and the bags under them sagged from the weight. "Oh, let me guess. A Diet Sun Drop."

Minutes later, a basket of chicken wings and a glass of Diet Sun Drop with shaved ice are in front of me. I speculated about the man seated next to me. He was dressed in jeans, a denim shirt, and a saddle-colored corduroy coat. His hair was light brown and almost touched his shoulders. His beard appeared comfortable on him. I would wager that he had not been cleanly shaven for several years. He seemed to be younger than I am but not by more than five years. Periodically, he removed his small round glasses and rubbed them with a handkerchief. I decided that he must be a local teacher, maybe a professor at the community college.

He drank from his fresh beer. "My name is Ben," he said as he held out his hand.

I shook his hand and introduced myself.

"You must be the guy managing Howard's Marina."

"That would be me."

He shared that his wife was a professor at the community college, but he failed to mention his profession. She was out of town, and he loved Stan's chicken wings, which she would not consider appropriate dining. He confessed that as far as cooking goes that he couldn't make much more than toast, and he labored in that endeavor. He carried a genuine self-deprecating humor that downplayed the high intelligence that was perceptible without being exhibited.

He told me that they lived in Atlanta before they each decided to do with less and move to a slower pace of life. She was pregnant and they expected twin boys in four months. His voice never varied as he spoke of the sons that were to come, but his eyes reveled with anticipation.

A short, portly man with an unkempt beard sat next to me. He wore a plain fatigued black hat and a black and gray flannel shirt that had seen better days. He reminded me of the guy that was always at the bar on the Netflix show, *The Ranch.*

He ordered a beer with a shot of Jack on the side. He turned his attention to the game and began offering commentary to the television as if it could hear him. It couldn't, but unfortunately, we could.

Every few seconds, he offered a negative comment about a Duke player, their rat-faced coach, and what an elitist bunch of sons of bitches the whole school was. I tried in vain to tune him out.

The man drank steadily. He offered Dick Vitale unsolicited help on calling the game. As if Dickie V ever desired to share a microphone with anyone. Every time the refs blew the whistle on Georgia Tech, he cursed their stupidity and more their blatant bias for Duke.

Duke began to pull away with a barrage of three-point baskets. I sat quietly, trying to enjoy the game. I'd never cared much for the jawing back and forth over watching a game.

He became drunker and wobbled on the stool, and he brushed up against me several times. The last time he did it, his shoulder remained longer than I would prefer. I raised my elbow to clear space and get him off of me. He looked at me with squinting eyes. "Stay out of my space," I said.

His lips snarled as he said, "Why don't you just shut up?"

Before I realized it, my right hand shot out toward his chin. My butt lifted slightly off the stool for power, and he crashed to the floor along with his beer mug and shot glass.

I stood over him as it dawned on me what I had done. Stan arrived at the skirmish. He eyed me with an expression of perplexity. The bar was still. That's good for me. I'm still looked upon as a stranger and for all I know, this man could have friends here ready to take up his fight. The man on the floor began to shake his head. He looked up at me with a face etched with bewilderment and said, "You hit me."

I said nothing. No one moved. Only Dickey V in the background added to what the man just said, proclaiming yet another can't miss diaper dandy.

The silence was interrupted by a voice from the other side of the room. "Bout time someone decked your worthless ass." Laughter filled the room and people resumed drinking and talking.

Stan helped him to his feet. "Go home and sleep it off, Mike." He guided him to the door. Mike offered no resistance as he rubbed his jaw on the way out.

Stan returned and stood in front of me. "I'm sorry, Stan. I'll leave."

His eyes were stern, and I felt like a third-grader in the principal's office, a place that I was all too familiar with. His voice was low and as dry as beach sand that the sea doesn't touch. "Sit down, slugger, and have another Diet Sun Drop, and try not to hit the HD."

HD continued sitting as if nothing had transpired. He wiped his glasses and began eating another wing.

I broke the silence that obviously felt awkward only for me. "Ben, how do you eat like that and stay slim?"

He put down a half-eaten chicken wing and drank from his mug. The man lived at his own pace. The world could revolve as it pleased.

"Good metabolism," he replied before adding a slight smile. "And I run five miles a day, four times a week."

"I run as well. Maybe not five miles each time. More like thirty minutes most days and forty-five on a good day."

"Thirty minutes is five miles for some people."

"I'm not one of those people."

"Neither am I."

The game in which I had lost interest in ends with Duke winning easily.

Ben beckoned to Stan. Without looking at a ticket, Stan said, "Call it nineteen bucks even, HD."

HD placed two twenties on the counter. "This should take care of the aspiring Heavyweight Champ beside me."

"That's a good one, HD," Stan said with a chuckle. "Yes sir, that's a good one," he repeated as he walked to the cash register.

"You don't need to do that. Let me help out with the bill," I said as I reached into my pocket for money.

He stood to leave. "Forget it," he said with a slight wave of his hand.

"I'll walk out with you," I said.

"Good idea. In case you need back up from Mike." There was a glimmer of humor in his eyes.

"Hey, slugger," Stan called out, which would be my given name from this night forward in the bar, "Duke plays Saturday night. I'll see you then."

The night was warm with a slight breeze. The moon was crescent-shaped but still offered ample light on a night void of clouds. Ben and I shook hands, and he walked away in the opposite direction of the parking lot.

"You need a ride?"

He turned back. "No. I live a few blocks that way," he said as he pointed. He took another step and turned back again. "Trent, do you know where the little gas station is that way?" he asked, pointing in the same direction.

"Yes."

"I start my run from there in the mornings. I will be there at 7." He departed without waiting for a response.

The next morning, we ran five miles in forty-five minutes. He was one of those effortless runners that I envied. His feet touched the pavement as lightly as a feather landing on the ground. I, on the other hand, always felt like a plodder. I must sound like an overweight horse coming up behind someone.

We finished and I was drenched in sweat. Ben appeared as if he had been out for a leisurely drive.

"Walk with me to my house, and we'll get some water."

We walked two blocks up a slight hill. The neighborhood was old, with mature trees, and homes that were probably built over a half-century ago. His home was a one-story house with white brick. The inside was tidy, and the floors were hardwoods that appeared to have been recently refinished. He gave me a bottle of water and excused himself to the bathroom.

The night before had bothered me, though he did not mention it this morning. I hit someone. I worked as a bouncer for two summers at Wrightsville Beach and managed to never hit anyone.

I roamed around the living room and looked at all the pictures displayed on the walls. His wife was an attractive woman, small, petite, and in each picture, her smile granted a soft glow to her face.

"Will you have to return home to shower?" he asked, startling me from my observations.

"No. There is a shower in the office. I packed a change for work."

"I run Monday, Tuesday, Thursday, and Saturday. Same time, rain or shine. Join me whenever you feel like it."

"I don't usually hit people."

He nodded and said nothing, not taken aback in the least at my abrupt change of subjects.

I forced a laugh. "You know he could have called me any name, and I would not have flinched, but I grew up with a father who never cared what I had to say about anything. I thought that my name was shut up until I was sixteen. There is not much you can say to me that provokes the response that shut up does. I just normally don't hit someone."

He listened and then asked, "You heard me about the running times, right?"

"Yes." I wondered if he had heard what I just said or heard it and had no interest.

"Thanks for the water. I'll probably show up occasionally to run with you."

I was almost to the door. I turned back. "Why does Stan call you HD?"

"I'm a psychologist."

It took a moment to register, but then Stan's sense of humor became clear.

"HD is for Head Doctor." I shook my head slightly and looked at the floor.

He took a card from the basket in the kitchen and walked toward me. Extending it to me he said, "If you want to come by my office and talk sometime, call me. Regardless, you are welcome to run with me anytime."

The rattling of ice cubes in the glass startled me from HD to the present. "That was probably more info than you needed, Jackson."

"Did you go see him?"

I nodded.

"And?"

"And what?"

"What became of it?"

I breathed deeply.

When I failed to continue, he asked, "So, what was the verdict?"

"We got to get you a woman, Jackson. You are far too interested in my life."

I could taste the salt from the ocean on my lips. I drank to wash it away. "I learned about brick walls."

When I failed to continue, he asked, "What brick walls?"

"The ones that I kept ramming my head into."

"Like Carmen and Alex?"

"Yes, and with my family. It wasn't that what he said was a revelation. I always knew it, but I did not live my life with the acceptance of it.

"He asked me all these questions about my family and when it was complete, he said, 'You don't measure up.' He used one of those psycho terms." I paused, the words escaping me for a moment in the haze of alcohol. "Oh, identified patient."

I drank from my glass. "I hated that word, and I got pissed at him. He told me that it was how they viewed me. And that it didn't matter. What mattered was how I viewed myself."

"HD sounds pretty wise."

"He is. There is no judgment in the man. One day I was explaining this vision I had during the last bout of depression."

"Tell it to me."

"It is a deep tight hole. There were these huge rope-like vines that are there for me to ascend. It was pitch black at the bottom, and as I climbed near the top, the black faded to shades of gray. I told HD I could get to the top, where it was light gray. I knew that there was light above the hole, but I kept getting stuck and could not push through that last step. He said not to force my way. To wait and when it was time, I would emerge. Is this too much for you?" I said, interrupting my own story.

"No. I always knew you were strange. Keep going."

"I finished my story, and then Ben said, "When I was depressed, what I saw was—" It was not important what he described but listening to him, I knew that he had seen the blackness. Until that point, I tuned him out at times. I mean, how could someone help me if they don't understand that feeling of despair.

"Anyway, what he said about my family was pretty basic, that they don't care for my input on most topics. Your mom was your biggest supporter but even with that, she had her agenda, presenting to the world the close, loving family she longed for you all to be.

"He said I needed to accept that the approval of my family may never happen. I knew that already and for the most part, it had not mattered. But periodically, I would make the mistake of trying to explain something to them that was important to me. They just nodded their heads and say, yeah, yeah, but I knew I was being tuned out. I have to accept that while they love me, they are a brick wall, and it is best for me to stop when I get near that wall and walk around it."

I raised my glass as a stupid symbolic toast to the heavens. "Damn humbling to find out that like everyone else, I am a product of my environment."

"And all this time, you thought that you were special."

I started to rise from the chair. "Now you got me intoxicated and made me share a bunch of psychological babble. Let's go home and crash. It's been a long day."

"One more question? What was the hardest thing that he said for you to accept?"

I slumped back in my chair and breathed deeply. "It was a question about mom. You know how I feel about her. I would walk through fire for that woman." I stopped speaking. My thoughts were lost in the waves that embraced the shore, stopping just short of us.

Jackson waited patiently. "I told him what it was like growing up. A dad that never spent any positive time with me. Being put down and never encouraged about anything. He asked about Mom's role in all of this and I said that we kind of gave her a free pass.

"The next time I went for an appointment, he reminded me of what I had said and that it was very interesting. He wanted me to say that she should have spoken up. I never even considered the possibility before that moment. Dad would have done anything to please her. Perhaps even if it meant being a father, but she was too busy pretending that every unpleasant thing in our family didn't exist. So, she defended him. Always telling us how much he loved us but just couldn't show it. He was a product of his generation. I grew weary of that tired, lame excuse, and I am certain that my dad would have been the same regardless of what era he was raised in. I realized, however, that it was imperative to her that she believed it.

"HD said that it was pretty remarkable that I could break the chain and be a loving father and that I should give myself a break."

I drank from a glass that contained only slivers of ice and the remnants of watery liquor and Coke Zero. "Of course, I left him. So, I'm no better."

"What did HD say about you contacting him?"

"Nothing. He left all decisions to me." I rubbed my eyes, trying to rid the fatigue. My words were heavy and slow as I spoke. "I'm wiped out, Jackson. I can't talk anymore. Let's go home."

"We better not drive."

Wobbling slightly as I got out of my chair, I said, "Gee, what gave you that idea?"

"I'll call my neighbor, Bob. His wife, Wylene, is the one you saw reading across the canal early in the morning."

"He'll come get us?"

"Either that or she will."

I tossed the empty liquor bottle into the trash barrel. "Do you think that perhaps they might have something to drink?"

14

The sun was bright. The rich blue sky impeccable. The warmth felt like an early summer day. Church bells rang in the distance.

I walked back inside. I brushed my teeth and hair, managing to use the proper instrument for each job.

I put on deep blue swimming trunks, packed a beach towel, and my Pat Conroy book into my faded black and tan backpack. I stopped and glanced at the backpack, and I recalled the day that I purchased it.

It was a Thursday night in October. Brooks was ten years old. We departed the next morning to spend the weekend in the mountains with my buddy Marcus, who lived in North Wilkesboro. Marcus and his identical twin brother Ed, who lived out west in Yosemite National Park, are two people that always made me feel better, more optimistic about life.

Ed was an avid environmentalist. His hair was long and there were usually a few whiskers on his handsome face. Marcus remained clean-cut, appearing to have just stepped out of his military uniform he donned periodically for the National Guard.

Marcus was climbing the ladder of a vast corporation. He worked hard and was constantly traveling across the nation. He made the most of his downtime, and he enjoyed getting away to the peaceful environments that his brother worked and played in every day. Ed was not getting rich making a living as an outdoor teacher at Yosemite. Still, he treasured the beauty that he eked out a living in and thwarted any attempts by anyone that would make him a captive of the corporate world.

Their hearts were warm, open, and their constant boyish smile invited you to a better place. They shared a special love for each other. I was blessed that they considered me a friend.

The first morning that Brooks, Marcus, and I were in the mountains, the three of us started the day early with a hike up Stone Mountain. Brooks was at the steepest part when he wanted to quit. Two men came up behind us and one gentleman, who was struggling as well, said, "Come on, young fella. We can't stop now. We are almost there."

Brooks pushed through his fatigue and walked the remaining steps hand in hand with me. We sat with Marcus on the ledge of a huge gray rock. It was the third weekend of October. The colors below us were so brilliant that we all, including my chatty son, sat without words for several minutes. We drank from the bottles of water that Marcus carried in his backpack.

The next afternoon we attended an outdoor music festival. There were several bands and during the day, my young son was asked to dance by nearly every woman in our area. I sat quietly and relished the fun that he was having. The festival stretched on to late in the evening when even my son began to wind down. He fell asleep on the ride back to Marcus' home with a smile etched upon his face.

The ensuing morning, we departed for home. Usually, the ride would have been tiresome and long, but the magic of the weekend swept us home with laughter and joy in what only seemed minutes instead of hours. Along the way, my son touched me deep inside when he proclaimed it to be the best weekend that we had ever spent together.

It was Mom's birthday, and we drove straight to my parent's house to join her party. We had only been there for minutes when my father, in typical fashion, did his best to crush our bubbly spirits.

Brooks was proclaiming to his cousins about how great the weekend had been. Dad stopped and looked down at him and asked him if he was hard of hearing.

Brooks shook his head no, and then my father proceeded to tell him he must be because he talked so loudly. My son dropped his head in shame. Dad retreated to his den. His good deed completed. Dad was a good honest man who many people in the community respected highly. That was what they observed. What I witnessed was a man who often reveled in cruelty that left scars for a lifetime. He did not savagely beat any of his children, but rather he crushed hopes, dreams, and spirits as easily as he ground out a cigarette on the floor with his boot. He did not realize the scars he seared on us, the obvious and the hidden. He was always too busy patting his own back for all that he had done for us, when in fact, my childhood might have been better served if I was a bastard child. The happier times of my youth was when his shift work meant that I did not have to encounter him for days.

I motioned for Brooks to come with me, and we walked out into the front yard. My sisters and I had purchased a sizeable Japanese Maple Tree for mom. Brooks and I began to dig the hole for the tree.

"He hurt your feelings."

He shrugged his shoulders. "Not really."

Mom joined us and chatted with us as we planted the tree. Minutes later, Dad walked up. He refrained from telling me how to plant the tree. At least in this area, he yielded to the fact that my years working as a Park Superintendent gave me a slight lead over him in the field of horticulture.

I struggled in my mind about confronting him. In our family, the tradition is to not say anything important directly to each other. On the one hand, I wanted to bust his ass for hurting my son's feelings, but it was Mom's birthday and maybe on this day, I should adhere to her wishes and sweep this under the rug.

"Dad, I don't appreciate how you spoke to Brooks in the house. He told me on the way here that it was our best weekend ever together. We are here five minutes, and you hurt his feelings." The words were out, hanging in the air, and they seemed to have appeared without my help.

Then an amazing thing happened. Something came from my father's mouth that I never heard once. Not when he chased me down the street waving a belt like a madman. Not when we were out of town visiting a family member, and he forced me to sleep on a wool couch when I was seven years old. I was allergic to wool. It, along with many other things, triggered severe asthma attacks. I begged him not to make me sleep on it. He cursed and told me I would not get asthma. At two that morning everyone in the house was awake because I could scarcely catch my breath. How wrong can a man be? Not wrong enough to offer any remorse and say that he was sorry that he was the jerk that made you sick. He just rolled over and went back to sleep. If I had died that night, he would have admitted no blame. You can say I don't know this for certain but I do, for I know the man and his inadequate ability to contemplate his actions.

"I'm sorry, Brooks, if I hurt your feelings. I'm glad that you had such a good time." It was a massive step for him, but he couldn't leave it there. The Mullins trait that he had fashioned so skillfully emerged. The characteristic of not being able to ever be entirely wrong.

He turned to me and said, "I really thought that he might be hard of hearing because some people that talk loudly are."

My voice was even as I fought to keep the anger from it. "That is bullshit, and you know it. You said the same garbage to me when I was a kid, and it hurt me like you just hurt my son. Don't you do it again to him. Ever."

My parents were quiet for several moments. Dad never could endure silence well. He walked away. Brooks and I finished planting the tree, and he began to water it. Mom departed. She would probably ask Dad why he had done such a thing, but later she would find a way to minimize or excuse the damage he inflicted.

Brooks looked up at me, a slight smile gathering on his lips and a twinkle in his eye that I can still see today. "He did hurt my feelings."

I looked at my son and gently nodded. We went home that night and watched movies and ate popcorn. The perfect weekend was tarnished by my father but only temporarily.

I told Ben about this during one of our sessions. He smiled, wiped his glasses, and said, "It was still a perfect weekend, maybe even more so. The memories of the hike and the concert may fade with time, but I bet what will remain with him all of his life is that his dad stuck up for him even when it meant going up against his own father."

There were tears in my eyes when Ben finished. He had a gift for making me see the good things I had done. As time passed by, I believed Ben's observation even more. I protected my son from my father. It was a gift that I needed desperately as a child and failed to receive. Now, I believed that time to be the defining moment of happiness in the greatest weekend that my son and I ever shared.

Minutes later, I sat a few feet from where Jackson and I drank and talked the previous night. The sea was a mixture of blue and green. The sun touched the sea and then broke into a million minuscule pieces of shimmering light. There was only a few people out. The sun hung over the ocean, bouncing its rays off the water in different directions. The sea was calm.

I could be in church now but it would not touch me like the scene in front of me. This was worship, for when I looked out at such a sight, I did find a way to believe that God does indeed love me. There was a shrimp boat that may be ten miles away or merely a mile. It was deceptive on such a clear day. I thought about the men on it, weathered men who derived their living from the sea. I wondered if they were in awe of what surrounded them, or were they merely concerned with putting food on the table.

I thought of Luke Hilton, a retired pastor from the church my parents still attended. He called me his friend. I don't understand why such a spiritual icon revered by so many loved me in such a unique way, but I know that he does. I heard it in the softness of his voice, the inviting gleam in his eyes.

Luke lived with his wife in a home constructed before Hurricane Hazel. They lived across the street from the sound with an unobstructed view. I could hear him saying, "There is a calming influence the water has over us."

Life was a merry-go-round, and soon nothing seemed new. We just kept hitting the same spots at different times in our lives, making us view those episodes differently and feel otherwise about them.

The place that I continued returning to was that life was not fair. Life does not even out. It had proven foolish for me to believe contrarily. Even as I accepted this, I know that at times I would cling to the hope that much like the shrimp boat fading over the horizon, my ship was just off the coast waiting to return to land and dock, validating the struggles of my life.

Perhaps it was as simple as God just longing for us to trust him. Maybe that was why he chose not to answer my cries of despair when I was immersed in blackness, and my fragile mind could not find a place of rest, or perhaps, he helped in ways that I couldn't see.

I packed my belongings and felt the warmth of the backpack against my back. I thought of Stone Mountain, the weekend I would never forget. I peered out at the sea again. It had conformed to more of an aqua color. It was a different phase of the same but continuously evolving beautiful ocean.

A smile engulfed my face. A God that granted me the Atlantic Ocean and Stone Mountain might just be on my side after all.

I would visit my father and allow these last days to play out as they will with no attempt to tweak them. And maybe tonight, I would talk to my son and try to explain why I had no choice but to leave.

I took a few steps toward the street before I turned back to the sea and looked to the skies. "Thank you." I walked away with a sliver of peace I did not have when I first arrived.

15

Jackson left a note that he was going out on the boat with his friend Herman. I sat on the front balcony and lazily read the newspaper. I browsed through the classifieds and even recognized the job my dad had decided I should apply for.

As far as work goes, I enjoyed managing the marina. Guilt washed through me, and I knew that Brenda had to be removed from my life. It would not be easy, but what was she going to do? Confess to her husband that we slept together? I also had to make things right with Moses and Maybelle. That might prove the more daunting task.

I finished reading the parts of the newspaper that interested me and walked inside. I changed into compression shorts and covered them with faded navy-blue gym shorts. I grabbed a pair of quarter socks and my Asics running shoes and returned to the deck. I slipped them on and stretched lightly. I walked to the road and began to run easily. I did an easy five miles and returned in time to shower, change, and head toward my lunch appointment.

I walked to the side entrance of the police station. On the center of the door, in bold letters, it stated Employees Only. I ignored this and pressed the four-digit code. I heard a click, and I knew that the code remained unchanged. I opened the door and walked a few steps down an empty hallway before turning to my right and entering the room that once served as the dispatcher's office.

There was an overweight female police officer seated at the desk. "Can I help you?" she asked.

"I'm looking for Hayden."

She rose and the chair squeaked with what sounded to be relief. "He's cooking. The kitchen is—"

"That's okay. I know the way. Thank you."

I walked a few steps down the hall and turned right. Hayden stood over a huge silver pot, stirring the contents and singing. He looked at me and smiled. "Trent, my boy. Lunch is just about ready."

I heard a door open and the noise of several people entering. Word had leaked out that Hayden was cooking. Men and women clad in uniforms representing fire, police, and wildlife passed by. They would eat a generous helping of food and be charged anywhere from nothing if the food had been donated, on up to the outrageous fee of $2 if Hayden had purchased the groceries.

Hayden served up two plates of chicken and rice. He gave one to me and took the other. I followed him to the office. "Food is ready, Verna."

The lady I had spoken with earlier scurried through the door and down the hall.

Hayden watched with amusement. "That's a great behind if you like two of them. Of course, maybe I shouldn't talk," he added as he rubbed his protruding belly.

I chuckled and walked to the soft drink machine across the hall. I purchased a Diet-Sun Drop and a Coke for him. We sat in his office and began to eat. He asked a few questions about where I was living and what I was doing. Mostly he talked about my father and how he wanted him to get well and come home.

"Your dad told me the other day that he hadn't put his shoes on but twice since Christmas." He looked outside the window and said softly, "He's a tough old bird.

"He talked about you all the time when I would visit him either at home or during some of his stays in the hospital. Sometimes, I thought that you had come home. He sure wanted you to."

We finished eating and discarded our plates. He shifted the conversation to the latest news in town. Minutes later, I rose to leave. "How much are you robbing people for lunch?"

He reminded me of my father when he waved his hand lazily as if he was dismissing a fly and without words rendered the answer to my question. "Thanks. It was great. Just like it always is."

It was mid-afternoon when I arrived at the hospital. Mom was seated beside his bed. I took the seat on the other side without words. He appeared to be sleeping, but even now there was a look of agitation on his face. It seemed he was seeking a place of comfort that was not attainable.

"He is glad that you came home," she said.

I nodded softly, acknowledging that I heard her. I looked at him as I searched my mind for tender memories. He was dying. Surely there had to be some collection of memories that will touch the inner workings of my heart. There were recollections, and some of them quite amusing, but none existed that would speak of a love that a father and son should share.

Right then, the memory that stirred my mind was ice cream. His mother lived downtown with Dad's sister. It was during a time when a trip from Sea Gate to downtown Wilmington did not take thirty minutes. His mother lacked the tenderness that mothers are supposed to have. The words Dad offered for her were similar to the ones he used for his father who died before I was born. They were middle of the road words that did not speak of glowing love or anger, only generic words that seemed to hold no significance.

It was Mom who always demanded that it was time to visit his mother. I was forced to accompany them until I was old enough to refuse and smart enough to be somewhere else when they departed. From the time I was ten throughout my teenage years, I wore my hair long. Dad hated this but for the most part, he did not care enough to argue about it. Frequently, upon entering their house, the first words from his mother and sister were, "Why don't you make that boy get a haircut?" They spoke as if I was not present in the room. They were interfering, rude, and nothing like the grandmother near our house that I adored. My perfect grandmother never once said anything about my long hair.

On the ride home, we would purchase ice cream cones at the Dairy Queen and eat them in the car. We never sat there and ate them because Dad was always in a rush to go someplace. Even if that place was home. It was in the same area each time, just a short distance down the road when he would pop the last bit of the cone into his mouth. I would still be licking my ice cream and yet to reach the cone. I was always amazed that he could devour ice cream so rapidly.

Even the ice cream story was invaded by bad memories. On the way home, Dad would sternly command, "You get a haircut tomorrow." I hated the idea of having to get a haircut, and I hated him for not telling his mother and sister to mind their own business.

He woke from his sleep. Mom was instantly over him. "Do you need anything?"

"Some ice chips," he said as he licked his lips.

She fed him ice chips until he raised his hand to signal that it was enough. His eyes located me. "Your mom's car needs gas." He had spoiled her so much that she does not know how to put fuel in a car.

"Okay."

"Check the tire pressure too."

I nodded.

We left soon after, and I followed Mom to a gas station near home. I pumped fuel into her car, which had a half tank of gas left. That was always my old man's empty side of the gauge. I checked the air in the tires. I looked at the sticker at the bottom corner of the windshield. "What's the odometer read, Mom?"

She was frazzled, and she struggled to understand my question. I touched her arm. "It's okay," I said as I stuck my head inside the car to read the odometer. "Leave the car outside when you get home. The oil needs changing."

"You can do that later. You'll mess your clothes up."

She was the opposite of Dad. He was in such a hurry that everything had to be done right that instant. Mom would tell you that you could do it later.

"My oil changing clothes are in the garage, right?"

"I guess so."

"Okay. I'll see you at the house."

I followed her home and went into the garage. I looked on top of the dryer that she seldom used. She was from a time when the way to dry clothes was to hang them outside on a line. Besides, God dried clothes without adding to the power bill. My old ragged jean shorts and a dark brown long sleeve tee shirt rested on top of the dryer in the same place they were the day I kissed her bye and drove away to a new town.

Twenty minutes later, the oil was changed and water was added to the battery and radiator. I parked the car in the garage and retrieved my clothes. I went inside, showered, and changed back into my clothes.

She was lying on her bed, sleeping soundly from the exhaustion of another long day. I stood in the doorway and watched. I thought of times when Brooks was little, and I watched him sleep. I wondered if Mom had watched me sleep when I was little and had our roles now evolved into a complete circle of life.

I took a throw blanket from the chair beside me and walked softly to the bed and covered her gently. I kissed her delicately on her forehead with the love of a man raised in the south during a period in which boys feared their fathers and worshipped their mothers.

I walked away, pausing in the doorway. Looking back at her, I felt the tenderness of my affection. Strangely, thoughts of Alex invaded my poignant moment. I thought of how she criticized me in the end for being too close to my mother. As I walked down the hallway, I whispered, "The hell with you, Alex."

16

Mom was near the trash cart by the end of the garage. She seemed unsure of which direction to take. She touched the trash cart and then removed her hand from it and turned to go back inside. She halted after two steps and was stationary.

I gingerly approached. I was a few feet from her when I called to her softly, "Mom."

She turned to me. Mom had always looked younger than her age but at this moment, she had never looked older. Her face was tormented, her eyes distant, hollow, and out of focus.

I held her arm gently. "What's wrong, Mom?"

"Bad news." And then she buried her head in my chest and wept.

She lifted her head moments later. I guided her to the porch, where we sat. She gathered her strength to speak. "The new doctor had a different kind of chest x-ray done. It showed a mass in his lungs. It's cancer. That is why he has lost so much weight." She shook her head. "He may linger for months, or it could be only days." She paused and took a deep breath. "I don't want him to suffer."

The lassitude on her face was the result of her last hope annihilated. She had accepted that he would not find his way home again. All the years they shared will be but a memory. I wondered what it could possibly be like to have someone you are in love with for nearly six decades and lose them.

"Does he know?"

She barely nodded her answer.

***

I entered his hospital room late that afternoon, and once again, his room was free of guests. He was more alert than he had been in days. "Lord, people have been coming and going all day." He told me about two of his golfing buddies that visited. "Talked me to death. My ears are tired."

I chuckled at another of his oft-repeated lines. I always took, 'my ears are tired,' to mean someone didn't allow him to dominate the conversation.

Our banter during the next few minutes was light as always. There was no talk of the death sentence he was issued today. A cardiologist from the staff that treated his heart condition for years entered the room.

He checked his heart and scanned the chart. "Looking better, Mr. Mullins. We will have you home in no time."

Dad's expression was puzzled, and I witnessed a flicker of hope enter his eyes.

The doctor was out of the room three minutes after he entered. Dad looked at me with a glimmer of optimism. "I don't think that doctor believes I have cancer."

As gently as I could, I said, "He didn't read the chart. He just checked your heart." I have just crushed my father's hopefulness as quickly as it surfaced.

"I'm tired. Okay, Son?"

I rose to leave, touching his arm. He looked at me, and I saw that he was unsure of what to say to a son that he had never understood. "Check on your mom."

"I took care of her car yesterday. The oil is changed, tires and fluids all checked."

"Did you gas the car up?"

"First thing I did."

"That's good."

"Get some rest."

He closed his eyes and turned away.

The doctor that had just left us departed from the room three doors down. My fury escalated as I approached him. "I hope you did a better job with that patient."

"What's your problem?" he responded arrogantly.

I was past him now, and everything inside of me said to keep walking. He's just another doctor with a God complex. I ignored those voices. I turned and walked so close to him that he took a step back. "You did not even read the damn chart."

"What did I miss?"

"He was diagnosed with lung cancer this morning. It's too far gone to treat."

His eyes shifted nervously. "Why are you so upset with me?"

"You gave him hope, you moron. He had accepted his fate. I had to crush that hope. I had to clean up the mess that you left behind."

"I'm sorry," he said as he turned to continue his rounds.

"But you'll still bill the insurance company, right doc?"

His walk paused momentarily before he resumed his rounds without replying. We both knew the answer to my question.

***

The sun was setting over acres of marshlands. The sky unblemished. Rays of the sun reflected on the narrow channels of water that knife in and out of the marsh. I told Jackson about my trip to the hospital. That was twenty minutes ago, and neither of us had spoken since. We nursed the Red Stripe beers that I purchased on the way here. Occasionally, I felt his eyes on me, and I know he wanted me to speak. There was a time, as he had stated earlier, that I never shut up about life, about hopes and dreams. I was so confident that a day would arrive and the journey of this life would even out and make sense. The catastrophes suffered would lead me to this wonderful place to spend the rest of my life. I was certain that it happened with Carmen and then with Alex. Between those times, I thought it would be about a writing break. An agent, a publisher would want to take a risk on an undiscovered talent.

Maybe that might be the break that made the most sense. It would be the only way to clarify a heart that fueled a mind that seldom knew a moment of harmony but so urgently craved slivers of peace. Perhaps it was the part of us that thinks eventually life will even out and make sense. But in the winter of my great darkness, after Alex shredded the hope of our life together, I let go of such ruminating.

My life became unimportant, even to me. I cringed at the memories of more enthusiastic times when I shared my aspirations with others. Most don't care but if we are fortunate a handful of people do. My mother stood firmly by my side, regardless of the foolish mistakes I made, and she prayed for me daily. The friend beside me who waited patiently for me to break the silence of the evening. Friend is such a sacred word, and we use it about people in such a generic way. There was an old saying that I believe. If you can count on one hand the number of friends you have, you are far richer than most.

My life had been too much of all or nothing. I opened the doors of my life too frequently, and then I sealed the doors on almost everyone. I overcompensated for my mistakes and hurt others along the way. Some did care about the details of my life. I had hurt the son I loved above all. How could he know what I know? That if I had remained, something would have occurred that would have damaged him far deeper. Maybe it is time to tell him all of the truth and see if he will allow me the privilege of being his father once again.

"Jackson."

"Yes."

"The last winter, before I moved away, there was a freak snowstorm."

"I remember." He reached into the cooler between us and opened two beers. He gave me one and sat the other on top of the cooler. "What made you remember that?"

I drank slowly from my beer. "That's just it. I don't remember."

"I don't understand."

"I've seen photos on my phone. But I can't recall any of it." I paused and he waited for my explanation.

"It's funny."

"What's funny? You've lost me."

"The depression had such a grip on me that winter. I don't remember snow. Certain things happened that winter, I can't recall, and you know I remember everything. It's so damn strange and unfair as well."

"Why is it unfair?"

"Snow couldn't hurt me. I love snow. Why couldn't it be the things that do hurt you that your mind erases from memory? Like Carmen and Alex, when both of them said the exact same thing to me in the end. That they just could not live out of their heart the way I do."

He offered no words, merely shaking his head and surveying the last remnants of the vanished sun.

"I have no idea why I just told you all of this."

He clinked his beer with mine and said, "Because I'm your bro."

I looked at him as if someone foreign had just taken his seat. "Bro? Who are you?"

We chuckled softly together.

"Jackson, there is something I need you to understand. People view depression as a sign of weakness when they would be better served to think of strength. Because they have no idea how much courage someone has to summon to find a way out of that damnable hole of blackness. Battling depression is not for the weak."

"You used to say beating depression."

"I'm not sure that anyone beats it. It's always a part of you. Always a portion of who you are, and it is not all bad. You learn from it. You read my manuscript and liked it. I will tell you that if I do possess some small gift for writing that it would not be possible without having suffered depression. I wrote that story when I was trying to get over Carmen. It was my escape. The world I lived in was cruel and devastating. I created another place to live in that was not so harsh."

His face lightened. "Remember what we use to say we were going to do when the big payday came?"

"You mean when you sold two dozen new boats in one year, and I got a best seller on the book market?"

"Yeah."

"We were going to drink beer and watch television all day," I added.

"And we would order all sorts of silly stuff that they advertise on infomercials."

"Do you think we can still buy that polish that the guy lit the car on fire with and then rubbed the damage off to a high gloss finish?"

"I want the knives that will saw metal and then slice a tomato easily." He paused, before adding, "You better get to writing."

"Sell some boats, bro." We laughed heartily and then the hush returned for several moments.

"You never told me about the snow before."

"I know."

I deliberated carefully my next words. "Jackson," I said softly. "If I call him, will he listen to what I say?"

He rose and patted my shoulder. "I'll call him. I heard the door open and then close. It was time to try and explain to my son why it was so imperative for me to leave.

17

The headlights briefly reflected in the water before the sound of Jackson's car registered in my mind. He was parting to retrieve my son.

As a young boy, I vowed that if I was ever a dad, my child would go to bed each night hearing how loved he or she was. There would be no speculation in their mind. Even with my exodus, I know that my son knows that I love him.

I never thirsted for fatherhood. The truth is that my son was the result of a futile attempt to repair an irreparable marriage. Still, from the first day the nurse placed him in my arms and I washed him with my tears; I loved him with all that my heart was capable of.

I heard the wooden steps creaking. I rose and walked to the railing. Several times I breathed deeply.

"Sit in the chair, Brooks." I heard Jackson say.

He did as he was told. Jackson walked toward the door. "I want you to hear this as well. You've asked a lot of questions."

"It's not my business. This is for family."

I smiled. "The bible says there is a friend who sticks closer than a brother. That would be you and you deserve to hear the truth of my departure. All of the truth."

He started to pull another chair up. "No. You sit. I'd rather stand." He nodded and sat in the chair.

"All I ask is please don't interrupt until I'm finished. Brooks, if you want to walk away after that, I won't blame you." He said nothing as he looked away and peered out into the darkness.

I breathed deeply. "Brooks, I was in Jackson's office when his buddy from Georgia called. That was when I knew I had to leave. It was my chance. I didn't intend to run out on you.

"What I need to tell both of you is what transpired the night before that. You remember, Brooks, when we left Alex's home that I stayed with Jackson until I left.

"Alex kept bugging me to get the rest of my stuff out of her condo. I just couldn't go back to that place, and I never wanted to see her again.

"Eventually she hired two guys from work. They dropped my things off in Mom and Dad's garage. I bought a bunch of beer and drove around drinking. It was about one in the morning when I arrived there and parked in the driveway.

"I should have just gone inside and slept in my old room, but I just had to look in the garage. Those boxed items represented yet another failure in a long line of them, and worse, my choice to love her hurt you, Brooks, and it drove me into the darkest pit of blackness.

"I was going through the things, and of all the stupid things that break the last piece of your heart, it was a damn ice cream scooper. You remember how she didn't cook, wasn't domesticated, and was always telling me how great it was that I had things like a microwave and a pizza cutter? One day, she jokingly said, if you get an ice cream scooper, I'll never leave you.

"I bought a three-dollar black ice cream scooper and took it to what was supposed to be our home. She..." I paused, before adding, "Oh, what the hell, I might as well tell you everything. She saw it and took my hand and led me straight to that ugly couch of hers and made love to me.

"I guess that cheap ice cream scooper was a symbol of all the screwed-up choices that I had made. I sat there and then it was like something picked me up from that concrete floor. It was like the snow I can't remember, Jackson. The next thing I know, I was sitting in my car drinking, but now I had graduated to liquor. I don't even know where it came from. I guess I stopped at the ABC store sometime during the night."

They proved a good audience. They had not so much as offered a whisper. Brooks was no longer looking off into the darkness. His eyes were locked in on mine.

"I made a decision. I drove into the garage, and I fell asleep while the car was running. It was like I was playing a game with myself. I was just resting, and if I fell asleep, well you know, but I knew what I was doing. I thought that maybe they would rule my death accidental. That way, Brooks, you would get insurance money."

"But you are here, Dad," Brooks interrupted.

"I woke. Maybe it was minutes, or perhaps it was hours later. I truly don't know. I was disappointed. I shut the engine off and got out of the car. My eyes fell on what had saved me. The window in the garage was broken. I went into the house and fell asleep in my old room. The next day, I asked Dad about the window being broken, and he said he hadn't even noticed it. I guess the fractured window saved the life I was trying to discard.

The next day when I realized what I had attempted to do, well, I was scared that if I stayed, I would die by my own hand. Brooks, I couldn't allow you to live with that. And the chance to go to Georgia seemed like my best shot of survival. I wasn't sure that I could make it, but I knew my chances were better if I left."

I turned to Jackson. "Get all the answers you wanted? Your friend is so screwed up that he allowed an ice cream scooper to send him over the edge. And my mom might have been the one to find me. What a selfish and worthless bastard am I?"

"You were on the edge. You just weren't yourself. The right amount of pain could do that to anyone," Jackson said.

"Brooks, I know that my leaving hurt you, but if I had followed through with my act, that would be a scar you could never be rid of. I thought it was the best way. Once I left, I just kept thinking you were ashamed of me and you were better off without me. I was feeling sorry for myself. I made a mistake. I made a lot of them."

The air was heavy, and all I could hear was our breathing. "That's it. That's the story."

"When did the depression finally lift?"

I looked at my son. "It came in waves. The last one was that first summer in Georgia. I had a few weeks where I was okay, and then I woke one Sunday morning, and like a black fog of death, it had rolled in while I was sleeping. But that was the last one. No more since."

"You should have called me when it lifted."

"I didn't feel worthy to be your dad."

He stood and faced me. "You took a lot from me. There is no one around to say, Brooks, you ain't got the brains God gave a grapefruit, or when I can't find something, I don't hear you say, if it was up your butt, you would know where it was at."

"Father of the year, that's me, always."

"Do you know why no one else talks to their kid that way?"

I shook my head.

"No one that I know has the relationship that we shared. I always loved it that we could joke with each other that way. I missed the insults maybe more than anything because they weren't for real."

He looked at me with those soft eyes and shook his head very slightly. "Now, I want you to listen to me. Never, and I mean never say again that you are not worthy of being my dad." And then he was in my arms. I was too drained to cry and so was he. We heard a sniffle from Jackson, just before he made an excuse to go inside.

We heard the door close, followed by the blowing of his nose. "What a damn sissy," Brooks muttered.

I playfully tapped his head. "Don't talk that way."

"It's not my fault. I've gone to shit in the absence of a father." And then we held on to each other tighter. Jackson emerged several minutes later. He was smiling at both of us. He placed a soft drink and two drinks of Crown Royal on the rail.

Brooks and I let go of each other. Jackson put an arm around each of us and pulled us in tightly. I kept waiting for him to release us, but he drew us in tighter.

I interrupted the tender moment. "Jackson, Brooks called you a damn sissy for weeping like a woman."

He let go of us, and just as I had done minutes earlier, he teasingly popped Brooks on the side of his head, and then he embraced us once again. In the stillness of that night, I will never forget his soft words. "I love you guys."

18

The emotional reunion of the previous night proved draining for all of us. Brooks spent the night and no one stirred before nine. That was especially unusual for Jackson and me, but for a teenager, not so much.

Jackson prepared a breakfast of eggs, sausage, and waffles. The mood was jovial as we ate out on the deck in the radiant sunshine. Each time that I looked at my son, his eyes were free from pain. We laughed easily and often, and it was as if we had never been apart.

Knowing him, he will rarely mention the events of the past days. He had the gift of youth for recovery but I also hope that it is a part of his demeanor. I believe he will always be one to bounce back quickly from the adversities that life will unquestionably toss his way.

It dawned on me that it was a school day. "What about school?"

He grinned and a mischievous look entered his eyes. "Well, I could go in late, or—"

"What the heck?" I said with a shake of my head. "Was your mom upset about Jackson picking you up?"

"No. She knew it was important."

He was quiet for a few moments before asking, "Are you going back when everything is over?"

I hesitated for an instant. "Yes, but it won't be like before. I'll come back and if you want to, you can stay with me this summer."

My answer didn't leave either of them with the choice they desired. I felt the brunt of Jackson's eyes bearing down on me.

"Jackson, I don't want to leave Howard hanging. I like where I'm living. The community is smaller. This place outgrew me a long time ago."

The bumper sticker on the back of Pop's truck boldly stated. If You Like Wilmington Now You Should Have Seen It Before You Got Here. I had to agree with that sentiment.

"I promise both of you that I will come home as much as I can. I'll come for the two of you, and I'll want to take care of Mom."

Brooks studied me for a moment before asking, "What about Papa? Have you made peace with him?"

"I am at peace that our journey is almost complete. No one won. You got a better side of him than I did, and that's okay. He just didn't know how to nurture or care about relationships."

"Why?"

"Mom told me that when his sister was nearing the end of her life, she said that their father was not nice to him. He forced Dad to quit high school to work with him painting. He paid him next to nothing. And he was an alcoholic. I have told you that I never cared for his mom. I don't think I ever saw the two of them hug. She was a woman who wore a sour expression like some ladies wear an ugly sweater. Maybe the nurturing gene in him never developed because he didn't witness any of it growing up. When she died, he did not shed a single tear but then I never witnessed or heard of him cry about anything.

"Mom said he could storm out of the house raising heck about something and return ten minutes later whistling, and fail to comprehend why she was upset."

"One story that stands out is the wool couch and how he could feel no blame," Brooks said with a sigh.

"And I cried one time because I stuck you with a pin."

"What?"

"I haven't thought about this in years. You were a toddler, and there was a little clip with a bear on it that your pacifier hooked to. It had a safety pin that would hold it to your shirt. We were in their back yard, and I was trying to hook the pin back to your shirt. I accidentally pricked you, and you started crying. I felt so horrible that I cried with you. Mom walked over to see what was happening and I told her what I had done. She picked you up and started patting you and talking sweetly and then she said to me, 'Son, if that is the worst you ever do. You will be fine.' Honestly, I felt like a bull in a china shop trying to care for you during those times. Maybe men don't arrive into this world knowing how to nurture and have to learn it. I won't excuse the scars Dad inflicted, but his upbringing sure didn't help matters."

Elton began to sing, bringing an abrupt halt to story time. I answered the phone. It was Mom.

She said good morning and then began to ramble. "Well, everyone else is at work." She stopped again. I smiled at her style of communication. She obviously wanted me to assist her with something, but she wouldn't ask the question directly. She always divulged information that was not needed. If I called and asked her what she was doing, she would tell me her day down to what she ate for lunch. Conversations have always proved entertaining. Brooks had mimicked her for years. His favorite is how she asks questions and then answers them before you have a chance. Did you go to church today? No. Has Jackson gotten married yet? No. Come to think of it, the answers to her questions were consistently no.

I waited patiently for her to get to the point of her call. "Connie, she went back home Sunday afternoon. She needed to go back to work, but I have her cell phone number if anything changes." She hesitated again. "Well, I guess I could do it."

"Mom," I said firmly.

"Yes."

"What is it I can help you with?"

"Oh, we're going to put him in Hospice today. Could you help me take his things? It's not much. You know, just his clothes, shaving stuff, and, he was wondering if you could shave him."

I waited for her to answer her question. She fell entirely out of character and failed to do so. There were times that I would have probably loved to have had a sharp object near the old man's throat. "Sure, I'll help you move his things but I can barely shave myself without getting cut. When are they moving him?"

"Right after lunch."

"I'll come over in a few minutes. We will take care of everything."

"Oh, you don't have to do that. I could get—"

She was babbling again. I cut her off quickly. "I'll be there in thirty minutes," I said firmly. I ended the call. Jackson and Brooks waited for me to give the latest information.

"He's going to Hospice."

Jackson nodded. Brooks looked at a pelican diving for breakfast out in the canal.

***

I stood in the den of my parent's home. Mom was in the bedroom gathering clean underwear and tee shirts for Dad.

Dad was a collector of things. Not keepsakes that may have sentimental value. I never witnessed him express sentiment about any object. He was a collector of anything free that he might use at some point in his life or pass on to someone else. He was not too proud to ask on every visit to the doctor for free samples of medications he was taking.

My eyes fell on the shelf above the television. There was one divided section of shelving that appeared to be a foot long and a foot high. It was full of various inhalers. I softly chuckled as Mom entered the room.

"What are you laughing at?"

I pointed to the inhalers. "You have to admire his optimism. He would have to live to be one hundred and twenty to use all of those."

She smiled warmly, and I patted her shoulder softly. "I wish he would make it that long for you."

"Not like this. I would rather let him go home." She touched me on the upper part of my back but as often is the case, she moved straight to the tender part of my heart. "Yesterday, he told me that he was tired and that he just wanted to go home and be with the Lord."

This information surprised me because my father rarely spoke of God. He went to church with Mom because it made her happy. My sister, Chloe, once offered that he only began attending church with Mom when all the children were gone or old enough to not have to go with her, and he didn't want her to go alone.

"He loves you children, but in his generation, men were taught not to cry or show feelings. That would be considered a weakness."

I have heard this theory countless times. My thoughts drifted to the Phipps boys, Rick and Al, that I grew up with. Their dad often put his arm around them and pulled them into his side and affectionately teased them. I never told a soul this, but those moments stirred something in me that I knew could never exist in my childhood. I envied my childhood friends.

The recollections made me feel on the outside of my life, like a spectator watching events transpire. Growing up, I never felt like I belonged anywhere. Even if my dad would have been like Mr. Phipps, somehow, I know that with the restless spirit that I arrived into this world with, I would still have ventured down the same reckless roads of my youth. Drinking too soon, graduating to marijuana, and then trying a multitude of drugs along the way. I guess I was fortunate to even be here. Many of those that I chased wrong roads with in my youth are no longer here.

I drove her to the hospital. Dad's room was empty. The ambulance was transporting him approximately one mile to Hospice, the last ride of his long life.

We gathered his remaining items. Mom was in the bathroom collecting his toiletries. She was carrying on a conversation that I think only God could understand. "Mom," I called gently to her.

She stepped back into the main room. "Yes."

"Are you hungry?"

"Famished."

"We'll stop for lunch before we go to Hospice."

She nodded quickly and returned to the bathroom.

We ate lunch at a small Italian restaurant. The waitress asked for her order, and Mom chatted about several items on the menu that sounded good. The waitress responded by asking louder.

Mom finally rendered her decision. The waitress walked away. Once she was safely out of earshot, Mom said, "I'm not deaf. I'm just old and frazzled." The first part of that line originated with her mother. The second line belonged exclusively to her. We laughed together.

After lunch, we took Dad's things to his new room. The room was nice, with a view of a landscaped garden with a large fountain. Behind the garden was a wall of tall pines, oaks, and maple trees that developers in New Hanover County had not yet managed to demolish.

Dad was more alert than he had been in days. He even ate lunch. He was talkative and it was good to listen to him. Mom watched him and smiled warmly, so grateful that he felt better.

I left that day, not thinking that the man in that room was going to die soon. But I would be proven wrong.

19

It was four the following afternoon when I entered Jackson's house. Elton was singing softly. I answered my phone and smiled at the sound of my son's voice.

"Dad, have you been to see Papa today?"

"Not yet."

"I think that you better call Mimi. I just called. She sounded so sad."

"Okay, I'll call her right now. Bye."

I ended one call and began another. "Mom, what's happening?"

There was silence for several moments as I waited for her reply. "He's sinking fast." I felt the absolute resignation in her words. "Did Brooks call you? Yes," she said, answering her question. "I hope I didn't hurt his feelings. I didn't feel much like talking at the moment."

She was watching her husband die, and yet she worried about her grandson's feelings. That was my mother, a woman of unmistaken compassion and grace.

"Who's with you?"

"Chloe, Lydia, and Linda."

"I'm on the way."

Minutes later, I entered the room and the man who was so talkative yesterday was still except for the slight rising and falling of his chest with each labored breath. I wondered if he did indeed love me as my mother insisted. It had been so long since it mattered to me and even now it still was not a subject of great concern. I don't know if that made me less than a good man. I could love with all the feeling that I possessed. On the other hand, after I found no flexibility on the other person's part to accept and love me as I am, I could effortlessly dismiss them from my life.

I turned my question around. Did I love him? There were good times shared by us, but I could not escape the man that never tried to understand me and without shame often brutalized me with his words. The damnable part was that it was his choice. He praised himself for all he gave, both real and imagined. He never recognized what he did not give, and far worse, he failed to see what he had taken. He had no real interest in understanding any of us. I think he knew the least about me, but perhaps that existed only in my jaded scrutiny.

I felt the eyes of Mom and my sisters. Yesterday, Mom had asked if there were any problems that I needed to resolve with him before he was gone. Her selection of words informed me that this subject must have come from my sisters.

Sorrow consumed Mom's face. I walked over and sat next to her. I felt her hand rest on my knee.

I looked through the door out into the hallway as I begin to speak. "Mom, several years ago, I asked Dad if he liked his George Foreman grill.

"Two days later, he showed up at my office. "I got something for you in the truck," he said. I walked outside with him, and there was a box and inside of it was the largest George Foreman grill made.

"I told him that it was really nice and that he didn't need to do that because I was going to buy one. And you know what he said to me? That he hadn't bought me anything in a long time and not to tell you because, 'she can't keep quiet.'"

I felt her hand squeeze my knee. Mom worried about one child ever thinking one was favored over another.

The nurse entered and we watched her go through a series of checks on him. She smiled kindly to us and exited the room.

"I'll call Connie," Linda said as she rose. "She should be almost here." She walked out of the room.

"Well, little brother, being it was the large Foreman grill. They probably cost a hundred dollars. I'll need a fifth of that grill."

I snickered, as Lydia's joke probably had soared right over our mother's head. "I wore the grill out a long time ago, but I will be glad to give you $20." And then she walked over and sat beside me. She leaned her head on my shoulder.

Connie sobbed as she entered the room. She walked briskly to him. She regained her composure minutes later. "He was doing so well just yesterday. That is what you said, Mother."

Mom failed to respond. "He was," I said. "We should have known. How many times have we heard how someone perks up and talked about how good they feel? And then..."

It was close to midnight when I drove away from Hospice. The poignant sounds of the piano from Counting Crows seemed appropriate for my emotional weariness. The piano was accompanied by the lyrics of "A Long December". I smiled sadly at the memories invoked by it. It was Christmas when Carmen and I split. This song always brought me back to that turn in my life. The previous Christmas, we had spent a wonderful, unimaginable week together. We shared the depths of feeling and tenderness that hung so thickly in the air you might swear it was visible. But by the following Christmas, her father had strategically inched his way into our relationship. A place I could not allow him to be. Carmen made her choice, and I was the one expunged. I was destined to lose from the beginning, but I was not wise enough to know it.

And it's been a long December and there's reason to believe

Maybe this year will be better than the last

I can't remember all the times I tried to tell myself

To hold on to these moments as they pass

I drove toward Wrightsville Beach. The words of Adam Duritz surrounded me. My tears flowed peacefully and evenly like a gentle Spring rain.

I walked up the stairs. Jackson was sitting on the deck and I knew that he was waiting for me. "Have a seat," he said as he rose and motioned to the chair beside him. "I'll get you a drink."

My body descended into the chair with the fatigue of the long day. Jackson placed my drink on the small table between the chairs and sat.

"Kind of late for you to be up, isn't it?"

"I thought you might need some company."

My thoughts drifted selfishly to the loneliness that had consumed my life. I desired that partner that would be present to share the triumphs and soften the trials of life. Maybe another man would look at my life and envy the adventures that my freedom allowed, but I admired the man who had a wife that looked lovingly at him after decades together. A woman who loved him joyfully through good times, and held his hand, his very heart, through the bad.

I had suffered great solitude in my life, even when I was involved with someone. Maybe if loneliness had not proven such a part of my life, I would not have ventured down roads cloaked in dismal shadows. It would not have called to me if there was love I could rely on waiting for me at home each night. No man ever desired that kind of life more than I.

I know that I should look upon the bright side of things. I had a son, a mother, and a friend who sat quietly beside me in support. I love them all but it was never enough to still the demons that twisted and turned their path through the recesses of my convictions.

20

I ran the next morning easily and effortlessly. I may have even been under an eight-minute mile pace, a time I hadn't achieved in years. Jackson again was waiting for me when I returned.

"Take a shower, and let's eat breakfast."

Several minutes later, we walked to the restaurant around the corner. We ordered omelets, shrimp for me, a western for Jackson. There was the white noise chattering produced from the tables full of people in one room as we sat quietly. I thought of our last visit here and Jackson so uncharacteristically becoming irate with me.

"I have a client today at eleven. It looks like a good chance to sell a new boat."

"Good."

"What are you going to do?"

"I think I will lift weights and go to the hospital, I mean Hospice, after that."

"If—"

"I know."

We finished breakfast and walked back to the house. Jackson left soon after.

My car did not turn left in the direction of the drawbridge that I had cursed thousands of times. I drove in the other direction, deeper into the island.

I stood on the porch of an old white beach cottage and looked out at the channel. One direction ran back to the Intracoastal Waterway and the other toward Masonboro Inlet. Scattered marsh banks of grasses broke the openness of the water. It was a spectacular view anytime, especially at sunset.

Luke Hilton opened the door before I could knock. His eyes, as always, inviting, concerned, and twinkling with what I believed to be the very light of God. I struggled to find good in the church of today, but the man in front of me was the best representation of a loving God that I ever witnessed.

"Come inside," he said gently.

We sat adjacent to each other, content in silence. I looked out at the water, amply viewed through the large windows. "Something very soothing about the water."

He offered a soft smile and said, "Jesus loved the water."

I thought about the evangelists on television. The men who felt the need to use their voice in a pronounced roar. Females dressed so tawdry that it reminded me of costumes in search of a Halloween party. And some who thought they could produce the spirit of God with an awkward cadence. The end result reminded me of a polka dancer attempting to dance to rap music. Ministers of today often appeared more thespian than preacher, and not very good actors at that. They spoke of all they gave God while they drove their Mercedes and resided in mansions, reaping the benefits of a desperate people. The man in front of me rarely ever raised his voice. I never once saw him pound a lectern to drive home a point. I guess he understood that hollering at someone isn't necessary to reach them.

I looked at him and our eyes locked. "Why?"

He waited patiently for me to elucidate.

"Why do you always love me so much? By church standards, I live in a perpetual state of sin. I'm a lost cause to most."

He moved an errant strand of his brilliant white hair from his forehead. "There is no pretense in you, Trent." His answers were always uncommonly short and to the point.

"Dad doesn't have long. Mom wants you to lead the funeral."

"Well, he is not gone yet. We can pray."

Now my silence spoke.

"I would be honored to do the service when the time comes."

"I know that Dad would want you to as well."

We sat quietly for several minutes and gazed out at the water. I rose, and he did also. We embraced and he walked me down to the last step. I was almost in my car when he called my name.

I turned back to him. "Yes."

"Don't give up on God in your life because I know for certain that he has not given up on you."

I nodded my head gently. He turned and walked back up the steps.

My eyes watered as I drove away. He had a way of doing that to me. He seldom preached anymore. He does not have the strength for it. And yet he still ministers better than any pastor that I know.

***

It was just past four that afternoon when I entered Dad's room. I walked to his bed and looked down at him. He was so frail. His legs always skinny were no bigger around than a beer can. He had lived a remarkable life in many ways. He worked the job he loved and found the woman that he loved. He knew nothing of depression and misery. Despite my denigrations of him, he had achieved something few of us seemed to manage. He lived a happy life.

Linda's husband arrived, and they left to eat and to take a respite from the deathwatch.

I touched his arm and I thought of our times of shared laughter together. He could be thoughtful at times, as when he showed up at work that day with a George Foreman grill, or the many times that he helped me with a project at one of my homes. Maybe that was the only love he could express.

"It's okay, Dad," I said so faintly that no one could hear. "I forgive you."

I walked away. I hugged Mom and sat next to her. Family members chatted but I heard nothing.

Several minutes later, Lydia rose and walked over to him. She turned back to us. Tears streamed down her face and fell to the white tile below. "He's gone," she managed to whisper.

Chloe walked into the hall and located the nurse. She came in and put the stethoscope to his chest. She removed it from her ears and turned to us. She touched her heart so softly. Her smile of compassion filled the room as she teared up.

"Mom, do you want me to call Catherine?"

"You can," she answered. Mom's best friend, Catherine, and she were sisters in every way but by blood.

I walked out into the courtyard that was in the center of the buildings that surrounded it and sat on a dark gray stone bench. I called Catherine and informed her. She thanked me sincerely three times for calling.

Next, I called Hayden. "Hello," he answered gruffly.

"Hayden, it's Trent. He's gone."

I heard him breathe deeply. "I was just on my way out there to see him."

"I guess he couldn't wait."

"How's your mom?"

"Relieved."

"Yeah," he said softly, and then he chuckled. "I went to see him that first day in Hospice. I told him to get up out of that bed and get home.

"You know what he said?" He continued, not waiting for my response. "Hayden, I am in Hospice. They don't bring you here to send you home."

Hayden got the plans for me when Dad returned to the hospital. He got his last joke as well. In my father's grand style, it was as usual when he wasn't trying to be funny.

I called Jackson, and the call went straight to voice mail. I ended the call without leaving a message; within seconds, Elton sang.

"He's gone," I said to Jackson. I don't remember anything for the next few minutes. At some point, the call ended, but I don't recall what else if anything was said.

I looked at a twenty-foot tall Japanese Maple, the leaves bursting with such a vivid shade of red. "Hayden, they don't bring you to Hospice to send you home," I repeated, laughed, and then my laughter turned to a deluge of tears.

I heard footsteps approach and a soft hand on my shoulder. "Are you okay?" Connie asked as she sat.

I nodded softly. She put her arm around me. "I do love you."

"I know.

"But you are just such a knucklehead," and then she giggled. I joined her in such a peal of freeing laughter.

We walked back inside to rejoin the remainder of the family. The door that led directly outside was open now. I heard the chirping of baby birds crying for their mother. Later we would debate as to who opened the door. It was no one in the family. Maybe the staff did it as a symbol of his spirit leaving.

Linda was already in full swing making plans. This time she had a good one. "We will meet at Mother's. Lydia, you order the pizza. I will go by the grocery store and buy the beer."

At that moment, I thought of *Forrest Gump* and his best good friend Bubba expounding on the shrimp business. I could hear Tom Hanks saying, "Bubba had a fine idea." So did my sister.

"Did you call Brooks?" Chloe asked.

"No, this is one best done in person." She nodded her agreement.

I hugged Mom and walked outside. The sky was brilliant blue and cloudless. Spring enveloped me. Trees and shrubs burst with new growth. The mother of my mom, my perfect grandmother, died on the first day of spring. Mom's father and brother, who died tragically before I was born, each departed this earth on Good Friday. Now her husband was gone in April. One day, we would joke about holding our breath for May.

Minutes later, I was in front of the house where Brooks lived with his mother. He must have seen me arrive because I was scarcely out of the car when he walked rigidly across the lawn. I could see in his deep brown eyes that he knew why I was here, but he did not want it to be so. I never spoke a word as I watched his eyes search mine and then surrender fully to the realization that his papa was gone. He fell into my arms and wept. I held him tightly, and I thought of all that dad had missed. And why? What was he so damn scared of? And then I mumbled, "The hell with it." It was his loss to be that way. I had a son, and I was grateful that he knew that he could sob into my chest and that I would hold and love him as long as he needed. "Do you want to go inside and get your things?"

He let go of me and nodded. "How is Mimi?"

"She is holding up well. It will be a while before it hits full force."

"Wait for me," he said.

"I was planning on it," I said with a smile as I leaned back on the hood of my car.

We stopped at a small store along the way. I bought Modelo because I feared that my sister would show up with her trademark Coors Light.

We entered the house. The mood was jovial. My sisters were all present, along with their husbands, children and grandchildren.

Linda saw me with the Modelo and watched me go to the fridge. I opened it and discovered Modelo. I turned back to her.

"Didn't trust me, did you?"

"You got me."

I looked around the kitchen area. Word was not out yet. It was not official in the South that someone has passed away until fried chicken was on the table. Tomorrow there would be, but tonight was a time for the family to unwind and celebrate my father's life.

We drank beer and ate pizza together. Hayden came by for a brief visit. Jackson arrived shortly after. We took our pizza and beers out to the brick porch that was privy to so many conversations over the decades. My thoughts drifted and for a moment, it felt as if I had never engaged in a war with depression. That I had never left Wilmington. The better parts of my childhood visited, as I recalled playing stickball in the streets and trading baseball cards with my friend, Rick.

Later that evening, Jackson, Brooks, and I sat on the deck and surveyed the landscape. Even Brooks was quiet for much of the evening. We drank beer quietly. Well, Brooks actually drank root beer. He asked if we could stop and buy some on the way here.

We heard soft voices and occasional laughter from across the canal. Wylene and her husband Bob were enjoying the evening with two friends. Wylene stood and held up her glass of white wine in our direction. She was wearing a red dress and black stiletto heels. The other lady was drinking red wine, and the men each held a lowball glass. At some point, we all raised a glass to each other. Even Brooks held up his root beer-joining the toast.

21

I was directed by Linda to sit between Mom and Brooks. The hymn, "In the Garden," played soulfully. I had heard my father sing the song a thousand times. He fancied himself a singer, and Mom prayed diligently for him to be zapped by God, become a Born-Again Christian, and sing in the choir. But Dad never had plans to sing in any band but his.

The family occupied two pews in the church that my parents attended, and I did as well at one time. We pulled together in my father's death, proving to be the family Mom desired.

Luke went first, and as usual, he was flawless. My brother-in-law, John, went next. He told stories about how Dad couldn't understand that with all of his education that he could not change the oil in the car. And worse, he paid someone to do it. He shared how Dad was puzzled to hear that he paid $200 for a driver to enhance his golf game when Wal-Mart surely had one that looked the same for $19.95.

I kept my arm around Mom and watched as she sat proudly soaking in the many tributes made to her husband. I only let go of her one time, and that was when my son broke down. His papa would not drive him anywhere again. Dad would never amuse Brooks again by reading signs as he drove. He never suffered silence well, and if it took reading signs along the way to disturb the stillness, he would do so. Brooks' favorite was the sign in front of the house they passed each day on the way to the middle school that he attended for three years. The crude, hand painted sign read, Fresh Shrimp. Brooks told me that one day in January when there was no fresh shrimp or a sign stating such that his papa read it anyway.

The final song played.

How can I say thanks for the things you have done for me,

Things so undeserved yet you did to prove your love for me

The voices of a million angels could not express my gratitude.

The song reached its crescendo, and I felt moved to do something that I had not done in years. I raised my right hand to the sky, to God, in that poignant moment. I glanced next to me and as I already knew, Mom's hands were stretched out in worship.

***

I spent much of the next few days cleaning out the garage. Hayden came by and carried away truckloads of old paint, conduit, and enough electrical outlets to stock a small warehouse.

On what would be my final night before I drove south in the morning, the family gathered for dinner at our childhood home. I sat on the outside of the events and watched my amazing mother do so well as the center of attention. I would tell her when everyone was gone that I would be leaving in the morning. There were matters that I needed to face. I did not know what awaited me but somehow, I would survive. I always did.

I walked outside and looked toward the main highway. There was a shopping complex where woods once flourished back when I was a young boy. I knew every path in those woods. The bittersweet memories thinking of the countless times that I sprinted down the path to my grandmothers.

"Dad," Brooks called softly, interrupting my thoughts.

I turned to him.

"You're leaving tomorrow, aren't you?"

"Yes."

He smoothed his hand over his hair, and I could not find the cowlicks that once were the focal point.

"It's okay for you to leave. Everything is okay. Don't worry about anything with us."

The heart of the boy in front of me is an indescribable gift. We walked back inside, and the conversation was about how great Dad was. There was nothing like death to elevate someone's status. I was reminded that three of my siblings said they were not sure that he ever really loved them. Such talk will not surface ever again. In death, he became what he could not be in life, a good father.

I drove away the next morning; leaving the two people I cherished most standing in my mother's driveway. There were tears everywhere.

22

I entered the marina office. Brenda rose eagerly to greet me. I held her arms and prevented them from encompassing me. "No more," I stated firmly.

"You don't mean that." Her eyes sparkled with mischief. I stared into her eyes, unflinching. The truth of the moment entered, and her assurance turned to rage.

"I'll tell my husband. You'll be out of a job."

I looked out the window. Howard was tinkering with something on one of the boats. "You won't have to," I said as I removed her hands and walked with purpose toward him.

After Dad's funeral, I had walked Luke to his car, asking him if we could talk. He nodded once and waited. I shared my adulterous behavior with him. He listened and when I dropped my head, cloaked in my shame, he placed his aged, gnarled hand on the side of my face. He gently persuaded my head so that I would look at him. "You are far from the only affair that I have encountered in my years as a minister. I have seen members, elders, deacons, even ministers fall to temptation. Your story is not over. I don't love you any less and God surely doesn't. My advice is to face it head on, Son."

At that moment I knew what I had to do.

Howard heard my steps on the wooden dock and turned to me. He rose and beckoned me aboard. For the past several hours, I had searched for the right words.

"I'm sorry about your father, Trent."

"Thank you." I sat in one of the soft chairs, and he sat across from me and waited for me to speak.

"I've been sleeping with your wife."

He studied me and said nothing. I realized that he already knew.

He peered off into the sea as if he longed to be out there on the water miles from land and this conversation. "You probably won't believe this, Trent, but we were happy once and in love. I didn't always cheat on her or drive her to cheat on me. We were in our twenties, and we had a beautiful son."

This revelation surprised me because they had no children. He stopped talking and looked back at me. A boat passed by, and the wake moved us gently. "What happened?" I asked.

"He was three months old. I came home from work. I was so excited each day to see my baby and my wife with him. I walked into his room, and she was seated on the floor. The look on her face was unlike anything that I had ever witnessed. She motioned to the crib. I touched him, and he was cold, sudden infant syndrome. No reason, no explanation. He was gone."

I rubbed my hand through my hair and tried to take in the magnitude of the story.

"She had a nervous breakdown. We moved here from Florida and tried to rebuild our lives. We could not ever get past what had happened, and she never became pregnant again. After a while, we stopped trying. She became the superficial person that you see now. I became an adulterer and a lush."

"I'm sorry, Howard."

"Did she wear you down, Trent? You don't strike me as the type of man to do this. I know that type quite well."

"I have no excuses."

"Why did you come back? You had every reason not to."

"I had to face you and own up to what I had done."

"What is it you want from me, absolution?"

"No. I don't deserve that."

He stared into my eyes. And I witnessed anger emerge and then quickly dissipate. He dropped his head. "You know something funny, Trent?"

"That you still love her."

He looked at me with surprise impressed upon his face. "You still see the young girl inside of the woman that you once loved so desperately and you can never fully escape that."

He shook his head from side to side, and then he located something in my eyes. "Where is she?"

"Dead. She died in Jackson's arms on a dark roadside. She had left my house earlier after pleading with me for forgiveness and one more chance. I refused."

He stared intently at me. I rose from my seat. He did likewise. "Maybe it's not too late for you to tell her about the young girl you still love."

He reached his hand out, and I took it. "I'm sorry," I repeated.

He nodded his head in tiny shakes.

We walked down the dock together toward the office. She was sitting outside. Fresh tears ran down her face, following the same path as previous ones. Her mascara smeared badly.

I went inside to pack my few things. I put them all in a copy paper box. I turned back, and Howard was holding her. Her face was buried in his chest, and he stroked her back as he held her. I didn't know what to do. I felt like an intruder. I didn't want to interrupt. I tried to ease past them.

She grabbed my arm. "I'm sorry," she said. "I'm sorry about your father, and I am sorry for what I did to you."

Through the wounds, I saw a glimpse of the young girl that Howard loved so long ago. "It was my fault," I said. She released me, and I walked past them.

"Trent."

I turned back to Howard.

"You don't have to rush your packing."

"That's okay. I probably need to move on."

Her arm was tight around his waist, and I knew that the love still went in both directions.

"Where will you go?"

"I haven't given that much thought."

"What about home?"

I shook my head. "As Thomas Wolfe once wrote—"

"You can't go home again," he interrupted, before adding, "I forgive you."

It was the last thing I had any right to expect on this day. "This job, this place, you Howard, saved me."

"Good," he said forcefully. "Now, I want one thing from you."

Hesitantly, I asked, "What?"

"I want you to forgive yourself."

I nodded my head slightly. "I'll do my best."

"I might be able to find another boat dock for you to manage."

"You don't have to do that." I paused before asking, "What will you do with this?"

"Sell it. I want to take a trip with a special young girl."

She looked up at him and their eyes met. "We'll be gone for a long time."

"I think that's a great idea. Good luck."

"I have an idea. Why don't you buy it?"

I looked at him curiously. "You know the business. You can make this work."

"How much?"

"$750,000."

"It's worth more than that."

"I know but I bought it when it was in foreclosure. I will still make a profit. We are selling everything and moving." There was not a moment of disagreement from his wife about all the new plans. She just kept holding on to him as if she had discovered something novel and exquisite.

"I don't have that kind of money."

"Borrow it."

I looked at him, saying nothing as I deliberated.

"You took a chance coming here. Take another one." He pulled his wallet out and removed a card from it. "Take this," he said extending the card. "Tell him that I said to make this happen."

I took the card and walked away. I had more apologies that needed to be offered. Maybe this one would fool me with the outcome like the one provided here, but I had my qualms about that.

It was almost two when I entered the grille. The same three men were huddled around the chessboard in the corner. They looked up, and then all eyes returned quickly to the game at hand.

Moses, as usual, for this time of day, was cleaning the grill. Maybelle was busy at the register, tallying the receipts. She looked up in surprise and then turned around and said softly, "Moses."

He turned to her with a light-hearted smile imprinted upon his face. I don't know that I had ever seen him smile before. But I suppose as it is in most things, Maybelle saw the softer and better side of him that he kept concealed from the world. His smile perished hastily when his eyes located me.

There was silence for several moments as I mustered up the courage to continue my apology tour. "I owe you both an apology. I was disrespectful, and I am very sorry."

Moses cocked his head slightly to the right, but he said nothing. Maybelle looked awkwardly at me, perhaps fearing her husband's reaction.

"I have no excuses to offer. I was sleeping with a married woman. And I did it on your property. I will retrieve my things, and I won't come back." I started to walk away.

"What happened in Wilmington?" I was surprised that it was Moses who offered the question.

I turned around, pursed my lips, and nodded my head tightly a few times. "I went home to bury the father that I never knew."

He stroked his chin gently as his eyes softened. "I had one of those as well."

I nodded my head. "I'm not a good man like you are, and I accept that."

"You told Howard what was going on?"

"I did."

"How did he take it? I assume you no longer have a job."

"He forgave me."

"Just like that?"

"No. It was anything but just like that." There was silence as I remembered that I had been asked two questions. "As far as having a job. That is still pending. He offered to sell me the place at a reduced rate. I am supposed to call his contact at the bank and see about a loan."

"Why would he show you such mercy?"

I shook my head. "I can't answer that."

"Did you ask God to forgive you?" Maybelle asked firmly.

"Yes, ma'am, though I know I don't deserve it just like I don't deserve Howard pardoning me."

"None of us deserve God's mercy, but we can still ask and even accept it."

"That last part may take me a while."

"You don't have to leave the shack until you're ready."

I observed a flicker of surprise in Moses' eyes.

"Thank you, ma'am, but that's not enough."

"What is it that you desire?" Moses asked as he studied me.

"You have never wanted me here."

"That's true," he answered without debate or expression. "But for some reason, my wife has hope for you, or at least she did until she found out about that woman coming here."

I closed my eyes and dropped my head. I didn't think another apology would render me any favor. Moments passed and I felt her hand gently lift my chin. Her wide eyes so expressive, so full of grace and empathy. Her countenance reminded me of my friend, Luke Hilton. "Don't drop your head anymore. We are all in need of redemption."

I thought of the mother I left, the father that I never knew, and the son who I hoped I could rebuild our relationship to a place that far exceeded what was before. The journey of the day broke me, and my tears began to fall. She cradled my head into her shoulder as I cried.

I heard her voice softly. "Shh, shh. It's okay," as she patted my back gently. Moments passed and I felt a powerful grip on my shoulder. "Maybe you should stay here."

I heard the cooler open and the clink of bottles. I wiped my eyes and whispered my thanks to Maybelle. I turned and Moses gave me a beer. He was studying his. I read the label, Southbound Mountain Jam. "It's one of those craft beers the distributor gave me to try. Let's sit down at the table. I think I have a way to get you some air conditioning before the heat and humidity take over."

I looked at him startled.

"I tried to sweat you out for two summers. I give up," he declared with a pronounced sigh. He leaned in with his beer bottle, and we toasted to something unspoken. Maybe to a day of unmerited grace and forgiveness that I did not see coming.

"What else did you leave behind in Wilmington when you first came here?"

"My son."

"Tell me about him and what drove you here," he said.

I began to share the unedited version of the events that drove me to Dylan Town. At one point, Maybelle brought us another round of craft beers, and she sat and listened.

***

During the next week, I made an appointment with the banker, and I had a good feeling that the loan would be approved. I'm sure that it aided my cause that the property and the boat slips were probably easily worth over one million dollars if I sold it the next day. But I had no intention of selling it. I was going to work and make it a success, and one day that attainment would be passed on to my son. I told Brooks that if he wanted to visit when school was out that I had hopes that there would be air conditioning. He did not commit, and I was okay with that. He had his own life as kids do at that age. I had missed out on so much these past two years.

On my last night in Wilmington before I departed, my sisters and I found ourselves outside, just the five of us. They began to offer all the aspects of why I should stay, and I just let them talk with no need for rebuttal. At some point, they realized their endeavor to be fruitless.

"We never spoke of Roger Jr. I think I was twelve when I found out from a relative that I had a twin brother that died seven days after he was born. I asked once and Connie, you said never for me to speak of it again, especially not to Mom." I paused before adding, "Maybe the family would have been better off if he was the one to live."

"Don't ever say that again," Connie said sternly as she shook her head. "None of us have ever felt that way. Not for one moment." My remaining sisters all nodded their heads in agreement.

Once again, Connie was in charge, but my tough, unyielding oldest sister offered consummate sensitivity with her choice of words. "Mom had a nervous breakdown after Roger died. We took care of you for the first three months before she rallied to the task. We decided to never speak of it again, and we knew Daddy would never bring it up."

"What did Dad do when it happened?"

"He went back to work," Lydia stated.

There was silence and at this moment, all of my tough older sisters had tears falling down their faces.

"I wonder what it would have been like to have a brother. Would he have loved me? What kind of brother would I have been to him?"

It was Chloe who answered. "Yes, and there is no doubt about that."

My face squinted as I could not understand the firmness in her voice.

"You were the only reason he lived for seven days," Lydia said before succumbing to a torrent of tears.

Linda took over for her. "In the hospital, he was hooked to all these machines. They knew he was in trouble from the very beginning. They found out from the first day he did better with you in the crib with him. Each time he began to fade, you would touch his hand. His heartbeat would rally until finally, he could rebound no more."

"There was no explanation for it," Connie said, but we all witnessed it. "Mom believed that it was a sign that Roger would be healed, and when that did not happen, her mind snapped. I think even Mom lost her faith for a season."

I just shook my head in tiny shakes trying to process all of this new information. And then I pulled them all in tight as we wept together.

***

Lately, I felt as if a burden had been lifted. Early in the morning, I even read from the bible that Maybelle gave me. Maybe there was still the hope of restoration for a flawed, scarred man, such as myself. This life was indeed a journey. I thought about the Beatles and all their songs that I loved. There was a time I would have said without pause that "While My Guitar Gently Weeps" was my favorite. But life being the excursion that it is, "The Long and Winding Road" seemed more apropos to my life.

Thoughts of Carmen and Alex still visited, usually in the early morning, but they no longer took up residence in my heart. They were like a bird delicately landing on a branch but only for a moment before flying elsewhere. I was finally free from the pain that the paths with them fashioned.

Still, on occasion, I thought of the two times I fell in love with Carmen. The curse was that our love found me too soon the first time. I was a boy, struggling to become a man. The second time it proved too late for her when the strength of her father's grip was matched by the fears and insecurities that governed her heart.

I walked down the dry dirt road for breakfast. The sun was up, and the sky was flawless. I watched two blue jays chase each other from one tree limb to another. A squirrel darted from the edge of the woods to cross the road and upon seeing me, froze, unsure of which way to go, before returning to the security of the woods. I stepped into the open landscape-the woods behind me. An electrician was installing a meter box on a new pole on the edge of the forest. Another man backed a Caterpillar backhoe off of a trailer.

I entered the store, and Moses did not grimace at the sight of me.

"Are you going anywhere today?"

"No plans to."

"Better park your car here. Your road will be torn up for a good part of the day." He paused and rubbed his jaw for a moment. "You should have better power by early next week, and that means air conditioning. That's a friend of mine outside," he said as he pointed. "He's going to dig the trench down the road for the new line. Some of it will still need to be dug by hand near the shack. We can bury the line today, so you will have a driveway. We just need to leave it open by the pole and around the house. I know the inspector, and he knows that I don't shortcut anything.

"Maybelle is going to handle things here while I work on this project. I have a grandson, Malachi. He should be here soon. He's a good boy and likes to earn a little extra money. He works at a restaurant over in Jekyll Island, so he knows his way around the kitchen."

"I want to help."

"I was counting on it. I also have a few men from the church. They will be here shortly to help."

"Wow."

"That is how our community is. We are old school here. Your neighbor needs something-you just do it, even if they don't ask." He paused before adding, "I have two guys who are going to install the air conditioning. It's a floor unit. They found me a terrific deal on a barely used one. It should be powerful enough to cool the place pretty well."

I started to thank him, but he cut me off. "Sit down and let's get you some breakfast. I don't want you fading in the hot sun trying to keep up with me with a shovel."

"I expect my rent needs to go up."

He breathed in deeply and shook his head. "That's what I think as well, but Maybelle said no. So that's the end of that."

"Do you mind if I make some minor improvements at my cost?"

"Such as?"

"I can refinish the floor. That old floor just needs a little love, and I can put some insulation in the attic. It will keep the power bill down."

"That would be smart because the utility bill will be in your name."

I smiled and added, "A coat of paint would not hurt the walls and ceiling either."

"Any particular reason that you want to do all of that?"

"It's the least I can do, and I don't mind working on it."

He slid a plate of bacon and scrambled eggs on the counter.

"Am I out of favors?"

He looked humorlessly at me, but I knew it was for show. "What?"

"Can I lift weights in the shed out back where you do?"

"Figured you for the fancy fitness club type," he said cynically.

"I think it's time for me to return to the basics of a lot of things."

He nodded his head. "Yes. Feel free. Do you have any other plans?"

"I'm selling my car and buying a nice used pickup truck. If I'm going to be the owner of the marina. I need something more practical than a sporty car."

"I got another grandson who is the manager of the Toyota dealership in Brunswick. He will look after you. He will do you right on your trade-in for your car, and that way, you won't have to sell it yourself. Be one less thing because you will be busy now that you are going to be a business owner."

I was eating and thinking about how much things had shifted between Moses and me. "The neighbors. How are they going to feel about you doing all of this for me?"

"You mean because you're white?"

I raised my eyebrows at him and he chuckled. "I don't care about the color of a man's skin. I just thought you were trouble."

"And now?"

"I have hope that you might not turn out to be a completely lost cause. Try not to disappoint me."

I smiled and asked, "Will I continue to be the only white person in Dylan?"

"Oh, why don't you get over yourself? My grandson, the one that sells cars for a living. Oh, and named after me, by the way. Moses met his wife, Melanie, when they were attending school at the College of Coastal Georgia. She has strawberry blonde hair, freckles and is way whiter than you. I love her like she was my child."

He pondered for a few moments. "There are no all-white families in Dylan, but there are a few interracial couples, like my grandson and his wife. Truthfully, there was a time I didn't believe it was right. But time has a way of changing how we feel about a lot of things. Love, real love. It knows no color."

"What about your kids, Moses?"

"Two sons, who both chose the military for a career. Army, to be specific. We lost Moses Jr. in Iraq. Samuel is stationed at Fort Bragg."

"I'm sorry."

Maybelle entered from the back. "I got this," she said to Moses. "Now go and take care of upgrading the power to that shack."

"Let's don't call it a shack any longer," I said.

They both looked at me, a question without words.

"*Home*. Let's just call it home."

23

It was nearing one o'clock, the last Saturday in July. The summer weather was dispensing its normal, excessive heat and oppressive humidity. I was repairing a loose dock plank. So far, I had managed to keep my head above water, and I had enough money left to eat at the end of the day. Not bad when all things were considered. I heard a crack of thunder in the distance, and I felt a refreshing breeze that offered a momentary respite from the sweltering heat. I finished the repair, and I heard a rumbling roar and saw a sharp flash of lightning streak across the menacing sky that was growing darker precipitously. The storm was moving in my direction at an accelerated pace. Severe thunderstorms and rain through Sunday night was the forecast. That sounded great. I could stand a break. I had not hired any help yet, and part of it was to save money, but the larger part was so I could learn all I could about the business. I could even back a boat to the dock flawlessly now. Jackson would be proud.

I felt immense gratification when I left the marina at the close of each day and drove home. I was asleep most nights before the light of day vanished. Some of that attributed to the long work hours and some because my mind had discovered an abode of rest.

It proved challenging to keep my promise to visit Wilmington regularly. I visited for a few days before the papers for the loan were worked out. When I returned, Brenda and Howard had departed, and the boat dock belonged to the bank and me.

I chatted with Mom almost every morning. She manages well, despite, as she put it, losing half of myself. She felt the need to tell stories about him, and most I had heard but not all. This morning she told me about a church-related gathering that they were at. Someone asked him to pray, and his response was that he did not pray out loud.

Often, I repeated some of his sayings back to Mom that we had both heard a plethora of times. I told her that I observed a woman yesterday that he would have said, "She ain't nobody's purdy thing." Another one often frequents my mind that I have used often. "Why wasn't I born rich instead of so damn good-looking?"

I shared with her about my visit to the hospital the afternoon of his first open-heart surgery. I was looking at him in his unconscious state when suddenly, his eyes flickered open. "Is your mama okay?" I nodded, and he fell back into a deep trance. He never recalled our exchange.

I believe that he might have been impressed by my adventure into the boat slip rental business. If he was alive and well, he would have probably visited by now and told me just how I ought to be running the business. Often wrong, but never, and I do mean, never in doubt. Still, there was a part of me that longed to see his old Dodge truck drive up so he could look over his wayward son's latest excursion.

I think that my sisters have accepted that I will return home but only for visits. I believe that they also observed new life in me that contained hope, and our family, as I suspect most families do, may have their differences, but it didn't mean that we weren't pulling for each other. Chloe called last week just to tell me she was proud of me and that she loved me.

Brooks and I talked often, and I hoped that he would visit for a portion of the summer, but he had not mentioned it, and I stopped suggesting it.

I gathered my tools as I felt the first drop of fat rain splatter on my arm. I had taken three steps toward the buildings when the skies emptied. I was soaked by the time I made it to the office. I was shaking the water from my hair when I heard a voice from the corner.

"Grass needs mowing out front."

After my heart rate lowered, I said, "Thanks, Jackson. You almost gave me a heart attack."

He laughed loudly with his signature guffaw that I could pick out among a crowd of five hundred people.

"Why are you here?"

"Thanks. I believe I will have a beer," he said, motioning toward the mini-fridge in the corner.

I retrieved two beers, opened them, and gave him one.

The rain produced a soft roar on top of the roof. I looked at the television that was on the Weather Channel. The entire states of Georgia and Alabama showed precipitation. The heaviest bands of rain were on us now.

"Looks like I might get the rest of the weekend off," I said. "Now, what are you doing here?"

"Picking up a boat in St. Augustine and taking it to Maryland."

"Why didn't you fly?"

"I decided to rent a car. I got on the road early. I thought I would stop and make sure you were okay, but I can see that you are."

I studied him for a more detailed explanation.

"You look happy, perhaps even peaceful."

Elton began singing, and I took the call. It was a customer calling from Atlanta inquiring about the weather. Can't he listen to Jim Cantore like everyone else?

The call ended, and Jackson shook his head.

"What?" I asked.

"Please get rid of that sad-ass ring tone. Time for something else, considering things are better for you. I know you like Bob Seger but damn."

I shook my head. "Elton John, fool."

He smiled and replied, "I know. I just wanted to see if I could get a rise out of you."

"But you're right. It probably is time for a change."

"What will you change it to?"

"A Long December."

"Oh, hell no. Not that sad Counting Kings song that you listened to all the time after Carmen and you split up."

I shook my head and chuckled. "I was just messing with you, and it's Counting Crows."

"That is what I said."

"No. You said Counting Kings."

He smirked and retorted, "Same thing."

"I think they might disagree with you. I deliberated for a few moments and then I smiled. "Running on Faith."

"Another Elton John song?"

This time I knew he was not trying to be clever. "Eric Clapton, you moron."

He pursed his lips and widened his eyes in mock expression. "I don't think that you should call your best friend a moron."

"I have learned how to back a boat into the dock. Maybe you can broaden your musical knowledge."

He smiled and we sat in silence for several minutes, just two old friends watching the rain dance upon the landscape. The steady rain was softer now. He stood. "Hate for it to be such a short visit, but I need to get to St. Augustine and check the boat out so I can be on the water time the weather allows for it."

I stood and embraced my dear friend. He pulled away and placed both hands on my shoulders. "It was good for you to come here, and strangely enough, it turned out well for Howard and Brenda. He called me a couple of days ago, and he said they were happy."

"I don't take any credit for that."

"I know but it is peculiar how things have worked out."

"Where did they land?"

Jackson laughed softly. "They bought a place in Cabo San Lucas, Mexico."

"Wow."

"He asked me how you were doing, and he said he hoped you were not being too hard on yourself."

"It's a process."

"I'm glad to see you are doing well here, and I have a feeling that things are going to get a whole lot better for you."

I turned my head and looked at him with a puzzled expression.

"Just a hunch." He walked away, disappearing into the rain.

I locked up and walked outside. I looked forward to sitting on the porch, enjoying the rain, and reading my latest book by Harlan Coben. Next year, when the busy season hit, I would hire seasonal help, but I was content to do it this way for now. I started the engine to my two-year-old dark gray Tacoma pickup truck. I don't miss the sports car, even for one moment. I no longer needed a fast vehicle to make my escape in. I was through running.

Minutes later, I parked in front of Dylan's Grille, got out, and opened the screen door. There were tomatoes, cucumbers, squash, zucchini, and green beans in the produce section. The seafood side offered only turned up coolers. All the fish and shrimp had already been sold for Saturday night dinners. But the seafood side was not completely empty. There was a dog by the coolers, lying with his paws stretched out in front with his head buried between them. His back legs were splayed out. He failed to acknowledge my presence.

"What's the matter, boy?" I walked toward him. He barely lifted his head as he turned in my direction. He was an Australian Cattle Dog. His body was mottled-red with flickers of white mixed in, and he had a beautiful red eye patch that consumed the area around his left eye. There were traces of blue on his snout, and around his other eye was a background that appeared white with gray mixed in. His chest was broad and his head a bit big. His amber colored eyes were steeped in sadness. He wore a black collar, with the name Sully embroidered in it. I cautiously offered the back of my hand, but he returned to resting his head between his paws and looked off in the distance for something misplaced.

"You are a handsome boy, Sully." His eyes flickered for a moment, but he remained in his position, staring out across the parking lot.

"It really is a sad story."

I turned around to face the source of the sweet southern accent. She was wearing faded Capri jeans and an Atlanta Braves baseball jersey. The jersey was navy blue with Atlanta written across the front in red letters, bordered in white. Below the letters was the tomahawk symbol, also in red and edged in white.

Her face was the color of caramel, and it carried an array of backgrounds, and all of them woven together made her exquisitely beautiful. She had full lips and the kind of long, thick, curly hair that you just desired to run your hands through. Her two-inch silver hoop earrings poked out when she pulled her hair back momentarily with both hands before letting go. She was carrying an extra fifteen pounds or so, but she carried them quite well. Her chest was ample and impossible not to notice. She was what one would refer to as a curvy girl, and for my money, her curves were in all the right places.

I realized that I still hadn't spoken, and her eyes that reminded me of the emerald green color of the ocean that day a few weeks ago at Wrightsville Beach were squinted in my direction. "You must be the white boy," she stated and pointed behind her, before adding, "The one living in that shack back there."

"Not a boy," I said without smile.

She pursed her lips. "Um, I guess not."

I extended my hand and said, "I am—"

She shook my hand firmly and said, "Trent. I know who you are. I saw you leaving one day as I was driving up. I asked Uncle Moses who that handsome man was?"

Like a high school boy, the main thing I heard was handsome. We men are a vain lot. "Handsome?"

She acted like I had said nothing for several moments, but then she added, in a faked low gravelly masculine voice. "And he said to steer clear of that white boy."

I nodded gently and said, "Yes, I suppose that he did, and with good reasons too."

She narrowed her eyes, unsure what to make of my last statement.

"May I ask you a question that is probably not politically correct?"

"As long as it's not a request for my phone number."

"I wouldn't do that." She arched her eyebrows at that one.

I shook my head as I fumbled for words, and then I breathed in deeply. She was still eyeing me curiously.

"You are naturally beautiful. I don't know," I said softly, my voice trailing off.

"Black, Cuban, Italian, and some white." She looked intently at me and then added, "That was your question, right?"

I nodded lightly. "I'm sorry if I said the wrong thing. I guess I forgot how to talk to a woman."

"I doubt that. What happened with the married woman that used to come through here?"

I breathed and exhaled so forcefully that there was a slight whistle. I shook my head in frustration. Is this what I would always be known for here in Dylan Town?

"I'm sorry. I won't take up any more of your time," I said, placing my hand on the door handle.

"Are you sorry for what you did?"

"I'm sorry for most of the decisions in my life," I responded tersely, before adding, "But I'm especially remorseful for that."

"Please turn back around."

I shook my head and slowly turned. "My name is Regina. Uncle Moses calls me Reggie as many folks do around here. Aunt Maybelle calls me Gina, also as many people do." She extended her hand. I shook it for the second time.

"You were serious when you said that you would not ask for my number. Why? Would it be because—"

I interrupted. "I could care less about the color of your skin or anyone else's. Moses would disapprove, and I don't blame him."

"And that is important to you? What Moses thinks or is it because he's your landlord?"

How did I manage to leave such a lighthearted conversation with Jackson and be caught in such an in-depth dialogue with a complete stranger? I looked at her for several moments contemplating what to say.

"Just tell me the truth."

I spoke quicker than my standard southern discourse. "Because what Moses thinks about me is for some reason significant, and I only care what a very few people think of me. I didn't seek or care about my own father's approval, who just died, but for some reason how Moses regards me does matter. I have made progress with him, and I don't want to bring that to a halt. So yes, you are gorgeous and real and genuine, and I would love to take you to dinner sometime and listen to who you are and what your dreams are, and why you are a baseball fan," I said as I pointed at her jersey. I ran out of steam, and my words floated out there like a balloon caption of a cartoon, but I could not expunge them.

"So, if I offered you my phone number?"

I shook my head.

"Because of Moses?"

"Yes."

"Care for an observation?"

"Somehow, I don't think that I have a choice."

She charged ahead undeterred. "Perhaps you always knew that you never really would receive your father's approval, but Moses' approval might be attainable."

I thought of her words and after a few moments, I nodded my head slowly in agreement.

"I have a scripture for you."

I smiled knowing that I was going to hear it whether I wanted to or not. I gestured with my hand for her to proceed.

"Psalm 40:2 *He lifted me out of the slimy pit, out of the mud and the mire; he set my feet on the rock and gave me a firm place to stand.*"

"Why that particular passage?"

"Your actions may have placed you in a pit but you can move beyond that and stand firmly."

"Maybe one day. It was nice to meet you and unforgettable." I turned and entered the store. The same three men sat, hunched over the chessboard. The pipe smoker was playing today, and he was relighting his pipe as he pondered his next move. They all looked up and said in unison, "Hi, Trent."

I nodded, smiled, and said, "Good afternoon, gentlemen." After my apology tour, things transitioned between Moses and me, to the point that one day he walked with me to the door and stopped at the three men and said, "This is Trent. I don't think I ever introduced you."

They all stood, shook my hand, and offered their names. My how things had changed here in Dylan Town. Who knows, maybe in the winter, when the boat business slowed, I might sit around the spool and watch them play. I won't take part because the only thing I know about chess is what the pieces are and how they move.

I continued to the back. Moses was cleaning the grill. I did not see Maybelle. "Please tell me that you saved your friend some pulled pork sandwiches."

"I don't have any Caucasian friends," he responded and then bellowed with laughter.

He continued cleaning as he said, "I thought the rain might send you home early." He paused and added, "Funny thing happened here about an hour ago. Young white lad wandered in here. He looked like he didn't know what to do, and Maybelle studied him for a moment, and she said, 'those eyes and the shape of your face. You are Trent's boy.' And you know my Maybelle, she pulled that boy into her chest and held him tight and told him how glad she was to meet him."

I stared at Moses. Afraid to move. He cocked his head to the left, and I followed his direction, and sitting in the corner at one of the square wooden tables was Maybelle and my son. Maybelle was smiling with a glow on her face that belonged to the angels.

My son stood and then walked slowly toward me. "I'm hungry," he said. "You're my dad. Buy me lunch."

I heard plates land on the counter, both containing pulled pork sandwiches with slaw, hush puppies, and French fries.

"I would have fed him, but he wanted to wait on you," Moses said.

I looked back toward Maybelle, and I noticed that there was more than a travel bag in the corner. I turned back to him.

"I'm moving here."

"Your mom?"

"Don't ask me how Mom feels about this."

"Okay, I won't. I take it that you have a plan."

"I'm assuming that they have a high school here. I can finish school, and then we can deal with college."

"There is a college—"

"College of Coastal Georgia. I know."

"Please do not allow my finely prepared lunch to become cold," Moses declared sternly.

We sat at the counter. Maybelle gave us two glasses of sweet tea. She joined Moses behind the counter, and they put their arms around each other and watched us with a smile of contentment. We began to eat, and I was afraid that all of this might vanish if I blinked.

"So?" my son asked.

"So what?"

"Do you want me?"

I shook my head and said, "What do you think?" I stood, and the boy who was becoming a man before my very eyes stood and faced me. We wrapped each other up in a tight embrace. I tried in vain to keep the tears at bay. The sound of my sniffling gave me away.

Perhaps life did fuse together at some enraptured moment and made some measure of sense or validated our toils in this frequently problematic filled life. Maybe it was not all that we desired it to be, but maybe, just maybe, it was sufficient, even abundant, in a cherished moment such as this.

I looked toward Moses and Maybelle. Sweet Maybelle, with tears streaming down her face and at the same time adorned with a huge grin. Tough, strong Moses wiped tears from his eyes without shame.

I heard shuffling from the front of the store. The men were putting their chairs away and pushing the spool against the wall. I heard one door close, and then the sweet southern sound of a slapping screen door followed.

We sat back down and continued to dine on the mouthwatering pulled pork sandwiches. No one spoke for several minutes as the rain continued at a steady pace. I heard a boat motor out in the distance. Someone did not take the storm warnings seriously enough. There was the soft hum the ceiling fans offered.

After lunch was finished, the four of us walked out together. We stood in the screened-in section listening to the thunder rumbling off in the distance. The rain was now falling at a perfect pace for parched lands.

Sully rose and stood beside my son, nuzzling his head against his leg.

"Who does the dog belong to?"

Moses shook his head and said, "Sad story." He paused, before adding, "He showed up here three days ago. We called the number on the collar, but no one answered, and then Maybelle searched online. Sully belonged to a young lady that lived in Jacksonville, Florida. It was night, and a drunk driver ran a red light and hit her right in the driver's side of her jeep. She was killed instantly and Sully was thrown, God only knows how far. Maybelle was able to eventually contact the young lady's parents, who live in Australia. They asked if we might help find a good home for Sully. I told them that we would." Moses turned and looked at Sully, still resting his head on Brooks' leg. "He has laid outside beside the screen door since I found him early that morning. I let him in here when the rain started. He hasn't moved much beyond eating, drinking, and going to the bathroom. He has shown no interest in anyone until your friend dropped your son off here."

"Dad, he walked to me like he knew me. I petted him and even told him to sit and down, just to see if he had any training. I told him, no, when I went inside, and he returned to the same corner."

I thought for a few moments, and then I laughed softly. "Maybelle, policy on pets?"

She smiled and rubbed Sully's head. "It's negotiable."

"We will need a pet deposit," Moses said firmly.

I nodded my head in agreement.

He whacked me on the shoulder. "I'm joking, fool."

I shook my head in dismay at being duped by him once again.

"We can keep him, Dad?"

I laughed because at this moment my becoming of age adult son had reverted to childhood with those big pleading brown eyes that I could never say no to. "Yes."

He knelt down and rubbed Sully's head, who nuzzled his face affectionately.

"Would you like to attend church with us tomorrow and come home and have dinner afterward?" Maybelle asked.

I heard Moses clear his throat.

"Shh," she said.

"Maybe it would be all right for Brooks to come," Moses added.

"I told you to be quiet," Maybelle said.

"Bossy woman," he responded, which earned him a pop on his shoulder.

"Sure," Brooks answered.

Moses placed his powerful hand on my shoulder. "The best singer in the church that you will hear tomorrow is the lady you were talking with a few minutes ago. She has a heart for worship and the Lord. You will steer clear of Reggie."

I did one long, slow, exaggerated nod of my head. And after a few moments passed, I began to smile. Moses looked at me humorlessly.

"I can't help it if she finds me handsome."

He narrowed his eyes, but I perceived a slight sparkle, or perhaps I just wanted to see it.

"Since you are her uncle. She and I could get together one day, and then we will all be family." I could not hold back my grin as I watched his head turn slightly, and his eyes narrowed to the point where they were almost closed.

"She just calls me that. I'm not really her uncle."

"Dang," I said with a shake of my head while still grinning at the expression on his face.

"Where's the closest pet store?"

"When you leave here and reach the intersection where you typically turn to drive toward your marina. Turn the other way and drive eight miles. You will see a farmer's supply place on your left. They will have everything you need. Tell the man at the counter that I sent you. He will look after you."

"Wait, you said, your marina."

"That's right."

"I like the sound of that."

"Being a business owner, there will come a time when you'll be moving on from here. A successful business owner is not going to want to live in a small home forever. Especially now that you have your son to take care of."

"I kind of like it here, and it's a simple life that will help keep Brooks out of trouble."

"Keep you out of trouble, you mean," Moses said with a snort.

"That's what I have you for."

I thought about something, and I subconsciously smiled. "I was walking in the woods around here last winter, and noticed the land over that way," I said as I pointed. "It had some old flagging tape and it looked like someone had planned to build there. It's good land, lots of beautiful hardwood trees."

I noticed that Moses and Maybelle looked at each other with forced smiles, followed by an instantly recognizable hint of sorrow in their eyes.

"Did I say the wrong thing?"

They both shook their heads. "What about the land, Son?" Moses asked.

"Dylan Town feels like home. If the business does well and assuming that you own the land, you might sell it to me, and I could build a home eventually. Maybe in time for my mom to come and stay a few times."

I waited for a retort from Moses but he smiled and shook his head with a look of amusement. The man that was so rooted in everything in this area merely said, "I know a builder."

"Lord, there goes the neighborhood!" Maybelle said in a raised voice, and then she giggled like a schoolgirl. The three of us turned toward her in disbelief. Her chuckles turned to a roar of laughter that she was unable to control. Tears started pouring down her face. As our initial surprise wore off, Brooks began to snicker, and then he was laughing loudly. Moses and I joined in, and I think it continued like that for five minutes to the point where we were all gasping for air. Sully, at one point, cocked his head to the side with a look of bafflement.

Finally, we regained our senses. Maybelle had one arm around Brooks and the other around me. I looked at Moses, and he nodded with a smile straight from a man of great physical stature, but I had come to know his heart to be the more significant resource.

There was silence as we all stood there watching the rain, and I think we were aware that a man's life had been restored and that I could not have gotten to this place without the three of them and my dear friend, Jackson. I could see his boyish smile as he drove southward, envisioning my son and me together. His words lingering that things were about to get better.

I felt more contentment at that moment than I could recall at any time in my life. And at that moment, I knew what Luke Hilton had once declared to be true.

God never abandoned me. I had rediscovered hope...even faith once again.

CPSIA information can be obtained
at www.ICGtesting.com
Printed in the USA
JSHW031953041122
32617JS00001B/47